"[U]nrelentingly tense, expertly riding the line between paranoid and horrifying."

—*JEZEBEL*

"This is a deliciously frightening novel. Reid has a light, idiosyncratic touch but never lets his vise-like grip of suspense slacken for a second. Once finished, you will be hard pressed not to start the whole terrifying journey all over again."

—*THE INDEPENDENT*

"A brilliant, well-constructed Hitchcockian tale with a huge creep factor . . . a straight-on crazy win."

—*THE HUFFINGTON POST*

"A deviously smart, suspenseful, intense, and truly haunting book with a fuse long and masterfully laid. . . . [Reid has] found a way to make us feel old fears fresh again."

—*THE LOS ANGELES REVIEW OF BOOKS*

"*I'm Thinking of Ending Things* begins with the unnamed narrator setting off with her boyfriend to visit his parents at their remote farm, and soon devolves into an unnerving exploration of identity, regret, and longing. Definitely frightening."

—*THE GLOBE AND MAIL*

"Will inspire readers to reread the novel immediately, to try to figure out just how it was done."

—*TORONTO STAR*

"Reid has written a superbly crafted psychological thriller, with forays into the metaphysical, which promises to keep you up at night on both counts."

—*MACLEAN'S*

"A genre-twisting novel, and one that is delightfully confusing. It's smart and it will keep readers guessing until the very end."

—*VANCOUVER SUN*

"*I'm Thinking of Ending Things* is an ingeniously twisted nightmare road trip through the fragile psyches of two young lovers. My kind of fun!"

—CHARLIE KAUFMAN, Academy Award–winning writer and
executive producer of *Eternal Sunshine of the Spotless Mind*

"I'm Thinking of Ending Things is one of the best debut novels I've ever read. Iain Reid has crafted a tight, ferocious little book, with a persistent tenor of surprise that tightens and mounts toward its visionary, harrowing final pages."

—SCOTT HEIM, author of *Mysterious Skin* and *We Disappear*

"Here are some near-certainties about *I'm Thinking of Ending Things*. Number one: you're going to read it fast. Over the course of an afternoon or an evening. The momentum is unstoppable—once you start, you won't be able to stop. And two: once you race to the end and understand the significance of those final pages, you won't be able to stop thinking about it. This novel will find a spot in your heart and head and it will live there—for days, weeks, months, or (in my case) the rest of your life. Yes. It really is that good."

—NICK CUTTER, author of *The Troop* and *The Deep*

"In a novel this engaging, bizarre, and twisted, it shouldn't come as a surprise that its ending is even stranger than the narrative route that takes us there . . . but it does. Reid's novel is a road trip to the heart of creepiness."

—SJÓN, author of *The Blue Fox, From the Mouth of the Whale*, and *The Whispering Muse*

"*I'm Thinking of Ending Things* is an utterly compelling modern Gothic that stakes its claim in the inner precincts of horror. Reid builds tension the way Edgar Allan Poe builds brick walls in his basement."

—WAYNE GRADY, author of *Emancipation Day*

"An addictive metaphysical investigation into the nature of identity, one which seduces and horrifies in equal measure. Reid masterfully explores the perversity of loneliness and somehow also creates a very entertaining thriller. I found myself yelling at the characters to put their feet on the pedal and drive."

—HEATHER O'NEILL, author of *Lullabies for Little Criminals* and *Daydreams of Angels*

"Smart, dangerous and spooky as hell. Iain Reid takes you on a harrowing road trip that keeps you riveted until the final destination."

—BRIAN FRANCIS, author of *Fruit* and *Natural Order*

IAIN REID

FOE

A NOVEL

SCOUT PRESS

NEW YORK   LONDON   TORONTO   SYDNEY   NEW DELHI

Scout Press
An Imprint of Simon & Schuster, Inc.
1230 Avenue of the Americas
New York, NY 10020

First Scout Press hardcover edition September 2018

SCOUT PRESS and colophon are trademarks of Simon & Schuster, Inc.

For information about special discounts for bulk purchases, please contact Simon & Schuster Special Sales at 1-866-506-1949 or business@simonandschuster.com.

The Simon & Schuster Speakers Bureau can bring authors to your live event. For more information, or to book an event, contact the Simon & Schuster Speakers Bureau at 1-866-248-3049 or visit our website at www.simonspeakers.com.

Manufactured in the United States of America

1   3   5   7   9   10   8   6   4   2

Library of Congress Cataloging-in-Publication Data
Names: Reid, Iain, 1981– author.
Title: Foe : a novel / Iain Reid.
Description: First Scout Press hardcover edition. | New York : Scout Press, 2018.
Identifiers: LCCN 2018005384 (print) | LCCN 2018007387 (ebook) | ISBN 9781501127458 (ebook) | ISBN 9781501127427 (hardcover) | ISBN 9781501127441 (softcover)
Subjects: LCSH: Married people—Fiction. | Psychological fiction. | BISAC: FICTION / Literary. | FICTION / Suspsense. | GSAFD: Suspense fiction.
Classification: LCC PR9199.4.R455 (ebook) | LCC PR9199.4.R455 F64 2018 (print) | DDC 813/.6—dc23
LC record available at https://lccn.loc.gov/2018005384

ISBN 978-1-5011-2742-7
ISBN 978-1-5011-2745-8 (ebook)

To Ewan

One has to be careful what one takes
when one goes away forever.
—Leonora Carrington,
The Hearing Trumpet

ACT ONE

ARRIVAL

Two headlights. I wake to the sight of them. Odd because of the distinct green tint. Not the usual white headlights you see around here. I spot them through the window, at the end of the lane. I must have been in a kind of quasi slumber; an after-dinner daze brought on by a full stomach and the evening heat. I blink several times, attempting to focus.

There's no warning, no explanation. I can't hear the car from here. I just open my eyes and see the green lights. It's like they appeared out of nowhere, shaking me from my daze. They are brighter than most headlights, glaring from between the two dead trees at the end of the lane. I don't know the precise time, but it's dark. It's late. Too late for a visitor. Not that we get many of them.

We don't get visitors. Never have. Not out here.

I stand, stretch my arms above my head. My lower back is stiff. I pick up the open bottle of beer that's beside me, walk from my chair straight ahead several steps to the window. My shirt is unbuttoned, as it often is at this time of night. Nothing ever feels simple in this heat. Everything requires an effort. I'm waiting to see if, as I think, the car will stop, reverse back onto the road, continue on, and leave us alone, as it should.

But it doesn't. The car stays where it is; the green lights are pointing my way. And then, after a long hesitation or reluctance or uncertainty, the car starts moving again, toward the house.

You expecting anyone? I yell to Hen.

"No," she calls down from upstairs.

Of course she's not. I don't know why I asked. We've never had anyone show up at this time of night. Not ever. I take a swig of beer. It's warm. I watch as the car drives all the way up to the house and pulls in beside my truck.

Well, you better come down here, I call again. Someone's here.

I hear Hen walk down the stairs and into the room. I turn around. She must have just gotten out of the shower. She's in cutoff shorts and a black tank top. Her hair is damp. She looks beautiful. Truly. I don't think she could look more like herself or any better than she does right now, like this.

Hello, I say.

"Hey."

Neither of us says anything else for a moment, until she breaks the silence. "I didn't know you were here. Inside, I mean. I thought you were still out in the barn."

She brings her hand up to her hair, playing with it in a specific way, curling it slowly around her index finger and then straightening the hair out. It's compulsive. She does this when she's concentrating. Or when she's agitated.

Someone's here, I say again.

She stands there, staring at me. I don't think she's blinked. Her posture is stiff, reserved.

What? I ask. What is it? Are you okay?

"Yes," she replies. "It's nothing. I'm surprised someone's here."

She takes a few hesitant steps toward me. She maintains more than an arm's-length distance but is close enough now that I smell her hand cream. Coconut and something else. Mint, I think. It's a unique smell, and one I register as Hen.

"Do you know anyone with a black car like that?"

No, I say. Looks official, like government, doesn't it?

"Could be," she says.

The windows are tinted. I can't see inside.

"He must want something. Whoever it is. They're here, they came all the way up to the house."

A car door finally opens, but no one steps out. At least not right away. We wait. It feels like five minutes—standing, watching, waiting to see who will step out of the car. But maybe it's more like twenty seconds.

Then, I see a leg. Someone steps out. It's a man. He has long blond hair. He's wearing a dark suit. Collared shirt, open at the top, no tie. He has a black briefcase with him. He shuts the car door, adjusts his jacket, and walks up to the front porch. I hear him on the old wooden planks. He doesn't need to knock on the door because we're watching, and he can see us through the window. And we know he's here, but we wait and watch anyhow, and eventually the knock comes.

You answer it, I say, buttoning a section of middle buttons on my shirt.

Hen doesn't reply but turns and walks out of the living room, goes to the front door. She delays, looks back at me, turns, takes a breath, and then she opens the door.

"Hello," she says.

"Hi there. Sorry to disturb you at this hour," the man replies. "I hope it's okay. Henrietta, right?"

She nods and looks down at her feet.

"My name is Terrance. I'd like to have a word with you. Inside, if possible. Is your husband home?"

The man's exaggerated smile hasn't changed since she opened the door, not at all.

What's this about? I ask, stepping out of the living room, into the hall. I'm right behind Hen. I place a hand on her shoulder. She flinches at my touch.

The man turns his attention to me. I'm taller than he is, wider. And older by a few years. Our eyes meet. He holds his attention on me for several moments, longer than what I deem normal. His smile moves to his eyes as if he's delighted by what he sees.

"Junior, right?"

Sorry, do we know you?

"You look great."

What's that?

"This is very exciting." He looks to Hen. She doesn't look at him. "I had butterflies in my stomach the whole way over, and it's not a short drive from the city. It's thrilling to finally see you like this. I'm here to talk with you, both of you. That's all," he says. "Just to talk. I think you'll want to hear what I have to say."

What's this about? I ask again.

There's something unusual about this man's presence. Hen's unease is visible. I'm uncomfortable because Hen is uncomfortable. He better start telling us more.

"I'm here on behalf of OuterMore. Have you heard of us?"

OuterMore, I say. That's the organization that's dealing with—

"Would it be okay if I came in?"

I open the door wider. Hen and I step aside. Even if this stranger has malicious intentions, I've seen enough to know Terrance is not a threat, not to me. There isn't much to him. He has an office worker's body, a delicate frame. He's a pencil pusher. He's not a man like me, a laborer, someone used to working with his body. Once inside the front hall, he looks around.

"Great place," he says. "Spacious. Rustic, unadorned, in a charming way. Lovely."

"Do you want to sit down, in here?" Hen says, leading us to the living room.

"Thank you," he replies.

Hen turns on a lamp and sits in her rocking chair. I sit in my recliner. Terrance sits in the middle of the couch in front of us. He puts his case on the coffee table. His pant legs rise as he sits. He's wearing white socks.

Anybody else in the car? I ask.

"Just me," he says. "Making these kinds of visits is my job. Took a little longer to get here than I thought it would. You guys are a long way out. That's why I'm a bit late. Again, my apologies. But it really is great to be here. To see you both."

"Yeah, it is quite late," says Hen. "You're lucky you caught us before bed."

He's so calm, relaxed, as if he's been here, sitting on our couch hundreds of times. His excessive composure has the counter effect on me. I try to catch Hen's eye, but she's just looking straight ahead and won't turn her head. I return to the matter at hand.

What's this about? I ask.

"Right, I don't want to get ahead of myself. As I said, I'm a representative of OuterMore. We're an organization that formed more than six decades ago. We started in the driverless automobile sector. Our fleet of self-driving cars was the most efficient and safest in the world. Our mandate changed over the years, and today it is very specific. We've moved out of the auto sector and into aerospace, exploration, and development. We're working toward the next phase of transition."

The next phase of transition, I repeat. So, like, space? The government sent you here? That's a government car out there.

"Yes and no. If you follow the news at all, you might know that OuterMore is a joint assembly. A partnership. We have a branch in government, hence the car, and roots in the private sector. I can show you a brief introductory video about us."

He removes a screen from his black case. He holds it up with both hands, facing it toward us. I glance at Hen. She nods, signaling to me that I should watch. A video plays. It seems typical of government-style promotion—overly enthusiastic and forced. Again, I peer at Hen. She appears uninterested. She's twirling a lock of hair around her index finger.

The images on the screen move from one to the next quickly, too fast to discern specific details or glean intent. People smiling, people engaged in group activities, laughing together, eating together. Everyone is happy. There are several images of the sky, the launch of a rocket, and rows of barrack-style metal beds.

When the video ends, Terrance tucks the screen away in his bag. "So," he says. "As you can see, we've been working on this particular project for a long time. Longer than most people realize. There's still a lot to do, but things are progressing. The technology is quite impressive and advanced. We just received another significant surge of funding. This is happening. I know some of this has been in the media of late, but I can tell you that it goes much deeper than what's being reported. This is a long time coming."

I'm trying to follow his logic, but I can't quite piece it together.

Just to be clear, when you say, "This is happening," what exactly are you talking about? We don't follow the news much, do we? I say, looking over at Hen.

"No," she says. "Not really."

I'm waiting for her to elaborate, to ask a question, to say something, anything, but she doesn't.

"I'm talking about the first trip," he says. "The Installation."

The what?

"The Installation. It's the first wave of temporary resettlement."

Resettlement. Like, away from Earth? In space?

"That's correct."

I thought that was more hypothetical, like a fantasy, I say. That's what this is about?

"It's very real. And, yes, this is why I'm here."

Hen exhales. It's closer to an audible groan. I can't tell if it's uncertainty or annoyance.

"I'm sorry," the man says, "but could I trouble one of you for a glass of water? I'm parched from the drive."

Hen stands, turns in my general direction, but doesn't make eye contact. "You want anything?"

I shake my head. I still have my beer to finish, the one I was drinking before the car arrived, before our night took this unpredictable turn. I pick it up off the table, take a warm mouthful.

"Well, here we are. This is your house. Very nice. How old is this place?" he asks when Hen's gone to the kitchen.

Old, I say. Couple hundred years or so.

"Amazing! I love that. And you're happy here? You like it, Junior? You feel comfortable? Just the two of you?"

What's he implying? I wonder.

It's really all we've ever known, I say. Hen and me. We're happy here, together.

He tilts his head to the side, smiling again.

"Well, what a place. What a story. Must be a lot of history in these walls. Must be nice to have so much space and quiet. You could do whatever you want out here. No one would see or hear a thing. There's no one to bother you. Are there other farms around here?"

Not so much anymore, I say. Used to be. Now it's mostly just crop fields. The canola.

"Yes, I saw the fields on my drive. I didn't realize canola was quite so tall."

It didn't used to be, I say, when farmers owned this land. Now, most of it is owned by the big companies or the government. The companies grow the new stuff. It's a hybrid, a lot taller and more yellow than the original was in the old days. Barely needs any water. These plants will last through a long drought. Grows faster, too. Doesn't seem natural to me, but it is what it is.

He leans toward me.

"That's fascinating. Do you ever feel a little . . . antsy? All alone out here?"

Hen returns with his glass of water and passes it to Terrance. She moves her rocking chair closer to me and sits.

Fresh from our well, I say. You won't get water like this in the city.

He thanks her and brings it to his mouth, drinking three-quarters of the glass in one long, loud pull. A small rivulet of water escapes the side of his mouth, down his chin. He puts the glass down on the table with a satisfying sigh.

"Delicious," he says. "Now, as I was saying, planning is already under way. I'm a liaison with the public relations department. I've been assigned to your file. I'll be working closely with both of you."

With us? I say. We have a file? Why do we have a file?

"You didn't until . . . well, recently."

My mouth is dry. I swallow, but it doesn't help.

We didn't sign up for anything or agree to have a file, I say, sipping from my beer.

He displays his toothy smile again. Like many people in the city, I assume his sparkling white teeth are implants. "No, that's true. But we've had our first lottery, Junior."

Your first what? I ask.

"Our first lottery."

"That's what you're calling it," says Hen, shaking her head.

A lottery? What exactly are you talking about? I ask.

"It's hard for me to know how much the general public such as yourselves are aware of already, how much you've pieced together based on things you've read or seen. I guess out here, not much. So it's like this: you've been selected. That's why I'm here."

Even though his mouth is closed, I see Terrance run his tongue over his top row of teeth.

I look over at Hen. She's looking straight ahead again. Why won't she look at me? Something's bothering her. It's not like her to avoid me. I don't like it.

"We have to listen to this, Junior," Hen says, but her tone is off. "We have to try to understand what he's saying."

Terrance looks from me to her and back to me. Does he notice her irritation? Could he? He doesn't know us, know what we're like together when we're alone.

"Excuse my informality," he says, standing up to take off his jacket. "The water helped, but I'm still a bit warm. Everything is air-conditioned back home. I hope you don't mind if I get a bit more comfortable. Are you sure you don't want some water, Henrietta?"

"I'm fine," she says.

Henrietta. He's calling her by her full name. He's sweating through his shirt. The blotches of random moisture look like a map of small islands. He folds the jacket and lays it down on the couch beside him.

Now's the time to ask more questions. He's giving me the opportunity. It's clear from his body language.

So you said I've been selected.

"Right," he says. "You have."

For what? I ask.

"For the trip. The Installation. Obviously, this is preliminary; it's just the beginning. I have to stress that this is still only the long list, so I don't want you to get too excited just yet. But what can I say? It's hard not to be excited. I'm excited *for* you. I love this part of my job more than anything—delivering the good news. There are no guarantees. I need you to understand that. In fact, far from it, but this is significant. This is a significant moment."

He looks at Hen. Her face is expressionless.

"You wouldn't believe the flood of volunteers we've had over the last few years. Thousands of folks are all dying to be picked. There are a lot of people who would give everything they have to be getting this same great news right now. So . . ."

I'm not really following, I say.

"Really?" he laughs, shakes his head, composes himself. "Junior, you made it! You're on the long list! For the Installation. If things progress, if you're chosen, you'll get to visit OuterMore's development. You might even get to be part of the first move. The first wave. You might get to live up there."

Terrance points to the ceiling, but he means to gesture beyond it, beyond the roof and into the sky. He wipes a hand across his forehead, waiting for his news to sink in, and then continues.

"It's the chance of a lifetime. It's just the beginning. We've gone ahead with the first lottery because this kind of . . . fortunate conscription . . . can take time."

I take another sip of beer. I think I'm going to need another.

Fortunate conscription?

"I know this is wonderful," Terrance says. "And it's a lot to take in. But remember, I always say this, and I really believe it: Everything changes. Change is one of the only certainties in life. Human beings progress. We have to. We evolve. We move. We expand. What seems far-fetched and extreme becomes normal and then outdated pretty quickly. We move on to the next thing, the next development, the next frontier. What's up there, it's not really another world. It is far away. It's been beyond our reach for most of our existence. But it's getting closer all the time. We're moving it closer. You see?"

His eyes are filled with a confident excitement. What do my eyes look like to him? It's not excitement that I feel. It should be. But it's not. I look to Hen. She feels me looking at her, turns, and smiles meekly. Finally. A smile. Something to unite us. She's with me. She's back.

This is crazy, I say, reaching out to touch Hen's arm. Space. It *is* another world. But we have a world here. A life. Here. Together.

I'm starting to feel defensive, protective of this life, the one I know and understand.

You show up here, at my home, I say, out of the blue, and you announce that I might have to go? Regardless of what I want to do? You think that after all this time living here with Hen, I might actually have to leave? I never asked for this. This isn't normal.

Terrance smiles again, leans forward slowly, cautiously. "Look," he says. "This is the warning." He stops himself, readjusts how he's seated on my couch. "No, sorry. That's the wrong word. *Warning* makes it

14

sound negative. And it's not. This is a good thing. It's a dream come true. And I admit that you didn't volunteer for this. Not exactly. But you have talked about space before. Our algorithm picked it up."

Hen perks up upon hearing this. "So you've been listening in on us?" she asks. "How long have you been listening to us?" There's an unfamiliar edge to her voice. It makes me feel . . . I don't know what it makes me feel. I just know I don't like it.

Terrance puts his hand out as if to apologize. "Please," he says. "I'm not being clear. I'm not explaining things very well. It's not surveillance or active listening. The microphones in your screens are always on—you know that. It's data collection. The program we use sorts through the information, categorizes it. It recognizes words of interest."

"I'm sure you'll be listening even closer to him now," Hen says. "Won't you."

"Yes, we will."

Hen's face is tight, composed, unrevealing.

Words of interest? Can you explain that? I ask. What kinds of words would have registered for the lottery, a lottery I wasn't even aware of, by the way?

I hope this is the question Hen wants answered.

"For our purpose, words of interest include any talk of travel or space or planets or the moon. We'd pick those up for sure. It's information we need." He stops, pausing as if deciding how much to say. "Our lottery system is complex and impossible to explain in a simple way. You just have to trust us. This whole thing is about trust."

Hen's hands are pressed together. She's so still, so quiet. Why doesn't she say anything? Why doesn't she ask more questions? Why is she leaving it all up to me?

Can you tell us more? I ask. What's the development like?

"Back when this started, years ago, there were many possibilities for human existence in space. Or so we believed. The moon. Mars. OuterMore was even considering colonizing a newly discovered planet that was orbiting a star in a neighboring solar system. In the end, we decided to build our own planet, as it were, our own space station."

All of this, what he's saying—neighboring solar systems—it's hard for someone like me to comprehend. But I have to try.

Why? I ask. Why build a station at all when there are perfectly good places to live here? And why build an entire space station if there are perfectly good planets out there already?

Terrance scratches the side of his head. "For lots of reasons. For example, if you were to travel to one of those planets, even if you traveled at the speed of light, which is impossible, it would take approximately seventy-eight years to get there and back. So that was a barrier. We chose to conquer other barriers instead. We knew we wanted the first phase, the development, to be a test period, an investigation. People would go and live there, we would observe, run tests, complete analyses, and then they'd return home. Building our own planet was the best idea for this model. There have been space stations up there. For a long time. Our first one was launched several years ago. We've been working on it since then. The development has expanded rapidly. It's now become a massive space station. It's orbiting around Earth right now, as we speak. It's not finished yet, but it's up there."

We can't help ourselves, I think, can't stop expanding, spreading, conquering.

And the government knows about all this?

"We are the government," he says. "We're connected to the government. It's our research."

I've never even been on an airplane, I say. Neither has Hen. She would hate it. She's never traveled far. She would be terrified of going to space.

"Oh," says Terrance. "I should have clarified that right away. That's my fault. It's you I'm talking about here, Junior. Just you."

And then it dawns on me. I see what he's suggesting.

We're not both on the list? We're not both part of the lottery? I ask.

"No, I'm afraid not. Only you, Junior."

Hen doesn't react. She doesn't say anything. She doesn't even sigh, or make a sound. She just sits there. I don't know how to take this. I don't feel like I have a choice. And she's not helping.

What happens next? I say.

"Nothing really. Nothing that's pressing or immediate. The list is still long, as is the process. Think of this as a marathon. It's part of our policy to give you this news in person, if possible. It's the best way to start our relationship. If you don't get picked for the short list, this will be our first and last visit, but it might be a lot more than that."

How long is the long list?

"Unfortunately, and I'm sure you can appreciate this, Junior, I can't reveal any details other than you're on it. Everything else is classified. What I can say is that nothing will be decided for a few years."

A few years. Hearing this helps me relax. This remote possibility is actually far off, distant, like the orbiting space station itself. Maybe Hen understood that from the outset. Maybe that's why she's so quiet, so calm.

This brings our conversation to an end, kind of. In actual fact, Terrance continues to talk, to pontificate, to explain the goals of OuterMore for another hour or more, but he's not saying anything relevant to me. When I interject with a question or comment, he toes the company line. A lot of what he says seems rehearsed. I wonder how long he's been doing this job. It can't be that long. He's still too scripted and self-conscious. It's clear that he's openly excited. That's for sure. At one point, he tells us about something OuterMore developed called Life Gel, a kind of topical ointment that helps bodies acclimatize to the lack of atmosphere. A gel, I think. A gel that helps you get used to something. It's so weird, so abstract, that I can't really imagine it.

When Terrance excuses himself to go to the bathroom, Hen and I are left alone at last. At first neither of us says anything. We sit in bewildered silence. Then Hen finally looks at me.

I look right into her eyes. Now that she sees me, is paying attention to me, I feel instantly better.

"What are you thinking?" she asks.

I'm not sure. Just trying to take it all in, I say, shaking my head. I know I'm supposed to be happy and excited, that this is an opportunity most people would pay for, but . . .

"Do you feel upset? Scared? Blindsided?"

No, no, no, I say. I'm fine.

"Good," she says. "It's a lot to take in. Fucking Life Gel."

Yeah, fucking Life Gel, I repeat.

Terrance comes back, so we don't have a chance to talk anymore by ourselves. He picks back up right where he left off, barely pausing. And yet, he still doesn't answer any of my questions. He goes off on abstract tangents. He reveals complex algorithmic details about the long list. He shows more videos of newly designed rockets with transparent exhaust and a video that attempts to explain something called "thrust vectoring."

Hen, sitting beside me the whole time, listens to all of it. Then, after a half hour or so, she excuses herself. Terrance talks at me for a while longer, and at last, it seems he has nothing else to say. I know I have more questions, more concerns I want to ask him about, but this whole experience has been so unexpected and overwhelming that I can't remember what my questions are. I've lost all my stamina, all my curiosity. I escort him to his car. We shake hands. Looking at him out here, feeling his hand in mine, I get an odd sensation for the first time tonight that he's somehow familiar to me.

He sets his case in the car, leaves the door open, and surprises me by turning back around and pulling me in for a hug. When he releases me, he steps back and grabs my shoulder.

"Congrats," he says. "I'm so pleased to see you here."

Do I know you? I ask.

Those teeth. That smile. "This is just the beginning. Day one. But I have a good feeling we'll meet again before long," he says. Then he settles into the car. "Best of luck to you."

The door closes with a thunk. I watch the car drive down the lane and pull out onto the road. It's pitch-dark out now. I can hear the crickets and critters in the canola. I look around. This is where I'm from. It's what I know. It's all I've ever known. I always assumed it's all I would ever know.

I look up at the sky—dotted with stars. The same as it's always been. I've been looking up at the same night sky my whole life. It's the only sky I've ever seen. All those stars. Satellites. The moon. I know the moon is so far away. It looks different tonight, though. I've never thought about it before, but if I can see it, all of it—those stars, the moon—see them from here with my own eyes, how far away can they really be?

The house is silent when I get back inside. Hen must have gone to bed. That's weird. She just went up without waiting to talk first? She's exhausted. That must be it. A stranger with strange news showed up out of the blue. I understand if she's tired.

I switch the lamp off in the living room. I carry the empty water glass and beer bottles into the kitchen and set them on the counter by the sink. I open the fridge, look inside, but don't take anything out. The cold air escaping the fridge feels good.

I walk upstairs in the dark, stopping on each step to look at the photos on the wall. I can't remember the last time I did this—stopped here to look at these photos. I have to get close due to the lack of light. There are three in total, framed and hung in a row. There's one of Hen and me together, and one of each of us alone.

The one of us together is a close-up selfie. It's hard to tell where it was taken. Hen's mouth is open; she's laughing. She's happy. That's probably why she hung this photo. In the one of me, on my own, I look so much younger. I can barely recognize myself. Did Hen take that photo?

I continue up the stairs and walk directly to our room. The door is closed. I don't feel the need to knock on my own bedroom door, so I slowly push it open. Hen is in our bed, lying on her back.

You're just going to go to sleep after that? I say. Don't you want to talk? That was crazy.

She brings her hands together, and rests them over her eyes.

"I'm sorry. I'd rather just sleep tonight. We can talk in the morning."

Are you feeling okay? I ask, stepping farther into the room. I see now she hasn't undressed. She's still in her clothes.

She raises her head.

"Actually, I'm not feeling all that great. I don't know, it's nothing serious, but do you think you could sleep in the spare room tonight?"

Really? I say.

I don't ever remember sleeping in the spare room. I never have.

"I know it's different, I'm sorry. It's just, if I'm sick or something, better that you don't catch it."

I'm not worried about catching anything.

Is the spare bed made up? I ask.

"Yes, I made it up this morning. I promise it's just for tonight. I'll feel better tomorrow. I'm sure I will."

Were you feeling unwell this morning? You didn't say anything.

"No, I just made the spare bed up on a whim, I guess."

We need to talk, you know, I say. I thought we were going to sit together, talk about everything that's happened, about what Terrance said, about the possibilities, about Terrance himself . . . I mean, what do you think of that guy?

"Junior, I'm really tired, so if it's okay, I'm going to try to sleep."
She turns away from me, onto her side.

Yes, okay, fine, I say. We'll talk in the morning.

I walk out.

But as I get to the door, I hear her call out, "Junior?"

Yes?

"Can you close the door behind you, please?"

Sure, I say.

I don't say anything about the room being hotter with the door
closed. That would only annoy her. Just before the door is fully closed,
I have a thought, a niggling concern. I lean my head back into the
room.

Oh, by the way. How did you know?

She rolls back over to face me. "Know what?"

When the car pulled up, before Terrance got out, you said, "He
must want something." How did you know it was a man in the car?

"Is that what I said?"

Yeah, it is.

"Are you sure?"

Yes.

She exhales loudly. "I don't know, Junior. It wasn't intentional. I
just said it without thinking. Good night."

Night, I say, closing the door.

It's not until I get to the spare room and look at the meager single
bed made up with clean white sheets that I hear the click of our bedroom door locking from down the hall.

W hen you get significant news, unexpected, shocking, potentially life-altering news, as we did when Terrance arrived, it has a peculiar effect on everything, especially on how you think and order your thoughts.

This is what I'm learning about myself.

For about a week or two after Terrance's visit, Hen was on edge, aloof, as she'd been during his visit. Out of nowhere, she suddenly wanted to spend a lot of time alone. We would eat together but talk little. She kept to herself. After his visit, she wanted to sleep alone every night and did so for almost a week. Eventually, she said it would be okay for me to return to our bed. But she felt tense. I could sense her anxiety beside me. It was palpable. I don't think she slept much at all. In the morning, she admitted to being awake much of the night. This went on for a while.

But slowly, she began to return to the real Hen, the Hen I know, her normal self. That's what time does. It ushers a return to equilibrium. Unease becomes ease. A shock, no matter how potent, always wears off with time.

Hen settled and allowed me closer. Life continued as it had before we received the news. Week to week, month to month. We've returned to our natural tempo. We work; we eat; we sleep. Life finds a way of balancing out. This is what we desire as humans—security, certainty, affirmation.

But it's my own private internal cycle, my inner world, that has been dramatically reformed, though no one can see that, not even Hen. Terrance's visit lasted fewer than three hours in total, not an extensive intrusion in terms of length, but disruptive and meaningful nonetheless.

Days turn into weeks turn into months. A year goes by. Another. We carry on.

But I think about his visit every day.

We rarely talk about it, Hen and I. When I bring it up, she usually changes the subject. I got the news about the long list and I started thinking about the future and what's to come, what may or may not happen, what it would be like in either situation, staying or going, the good and bad of both. I also started thinking about the past, my past, what came before, what brought me here. The big stuff. Meaningful memories that I hadn't thought about in a long time. Specific memories have been returning to me in waves. I have begun to remember the first few years that Hen and I lived here, what life was like for us then.

I wouldn't tell Hen any of this, of course. That's the deal I made with myself. Try to ride this out solo, if I can. Protect her. Let her forget. Just be myself, as though nothing has changed, as though everything is exactly as it always was. Even if it isn't. That's my duty to her. I don't want to upset or worry her. And that's what Terrance's arrival in our lives did. His brief visit rattled her. I try to pretend everything is the same as before, like everything is normal. I behave like all is well.

We get up in the morning. I go out to the barn. I feed the chickens. I walk around outside. I shower. We eat breakfast. We go to work. We come home for supper. Some nights Hen plays her piano. I drink a beer, maybe two. We discuss our days, recounting any funny or unusual occurrences. We do it again the next day.

One short, innocuous visit from a stranger, that's all it was. Why does it have to have such impact, such force? I've decided it shouldn't, that it doesn't have to. No matter what happens in the future, nothing in our relationship needs to be affected now. I should refocus on the present. We are a couple, like before. And it's my responsibility to simply be myself, to be who I have always been, for Hen's sake.

Nothing in our routine was altered or transformed. But, against my will, I feel myself changing. I feel myself changed.

The first time I saw Hen was from a distance. It's the clearest memory I have, the most intense, and the one I recall most often these days. I've been thinking about it a lot since Terrance's visit, playing it over and over in my mind.

No one else was around when I saw her. It was just the two of us. She looked so small. That was the first thing I noticed about her. I stopped what I was doing and I watched her. I cleared my head of other thoughts. I wanted to begin again.

It was summer, and bright, so I found some shade. I was thirsty but didn't have any water with me. I'd been moving for a while, hours upon hours, and I still had a ways to go. We were young then, kids, her especially. There wasn't much daylight left, and the weather was humid. Enough to make you slow down, enough to make it hard to think. She was wearing a white T-shirt with the sleeves cut off. She had her hair up in a loose bun with strands that had drifted down around her face. I sat in the dirt under a tree, on my haunches, resting my elbows on my thighs.

I didn't recognize her, and that surprised me. In a good way. Who was she? I wanted to know. I needed to know. It wasn't just that she was unfamiliar. That was part of it, but that's not why I sat in the dirt and stayed there, under that tree, waiting, looking at her. This is what I'd been waiting for. This was it.

I lit a cigarette. I pushed my hair up, off my forehead. It was damp, sweaty. I inhaled the smoke. I remember lying down then on my back. I stayed like that for a while, looking up at the leaves and shadows, branches and sky above them. Smoking. The whole moment was moving together, and I wasn't focused on any one part. She was beyond it all. But she was there. I didn't wave.

We didn't even talk that day. Not a word. There was no acknowledgment between us, but I felt a connection. I was on the other side of the road. I was alone. I thought I was alone. Until I saw her. She had no idea of her impact. She was oblivious. That was the power she had over me. Even then.

Seeing her made me question what I was doing, what I wanted, what I desired, what I could do. Not just in the moment. But what I had been doing that led me to this point, why I was there, out in the sun, my hands dirty and sore. My whole life, I could not remember anyone's name. Nothing had made a formative impact on me. But right then I thought that might change. If I knew her name, I would remember it. That's what she did, even before we'd met—she changed things. There she was, preoccupied, bent down, oblivious, washing her hands in a puddle on the side of the road. I knew she was the one. I was meant for her. I saw her, and right then, my life began.

Are some things meant to be, meant to happen? There are some things we can't explain. Some call it fate. Maybe that's okay. Maybe we don't have to know more than that. Maybe the orbit we inhabit is preordained. I'm okay with it even if I don't really believe in that kind of thing. You can hold beliefs and not always believe in them.

Later, I started to think about all the other possibilities that could have played out, how things could have gone a different way. Would I have seen her another way, at another time? On another day? Is any of this inevitable? You hear it all the time—meant to be. Was this the one and only chance? Make it or break it? Fate, or just coincidence? Was this the one opportunity? For me to see her, to take notice, to remember, to recall?

I had seriously considered taking another route. I can't even remember why I was on that exact stretch of road. I didn't have to be. Our fate seems as it should. We have found a way together, our way. We have developed and refined a relationship. Predictable, stable, certain, normal, routine, lifelike. One day ends, another starts. Over and over. It's a comforting rhythm.

I'm not an observant person. I see what I see, and the rest doesn't matter. What's the point? Why bother taking notice of everything going on around you, filling up your mind with irrelevant details and excess information? What's going to happen will happen regardless. Awareness is beside the point.

I wonder what Hen would say if I asked her about the day we met. Would she remember it? I don't know. And I'm not sure I want to know. But I wonder. The majority of our days blur together and don't leave us with distinct memories. Maybe one day I'll have the nerve to ask her.

She still has that white T-shirt with the sleeves cut off that she was wearing when I first saw her. I never told her its significance to me. She rarely wears it. I notice when she does. I'm glad that she doesn't wear it much, that it sits in her drawer. The more she wears it, the more she has to wash it, and the more she washes it, the more worn out it'll get. The material is already thin and frayed. It's stupid, I know, but I don't want her to wear out that shirt completely. I want it to last.

I t's earlier in the evening this time, but there's no mistaking it. I know immediately. Those same greenish headlights distinguishable and explicit in the fading light. I know them. I remember them. There's no waiting at the end of the lane. The black car turns in and continues up to the house without pause. I see him step out of the car, brush something off his pant leg.

It's been over two years since Terrance's first visit, two years and a few months, but here he is, returning to our quiet farm. Just like he said he might.

From here, he looks the same. Skinny. Delicate. The long blond hair. The suit. No tie. White socks. The black case.

A hard knock at the door. *Rat tat tat tat tat.*

I don't know if Hen's heard it, too. I walk to the door and open it.

"Hello, Junior," he says, beaming. "It's so good to see you."

Hey, I say.

We don't shake hands. He puts a hand on my shoulder and sort of half pats, half squeezes it. I move aside so he can come in. I see now that he has aged. Not dramatically. In small ways. His face looks even thinner than before, harsher. His eyes heavier. There's something rodent-like about Terrance. Not just his face, but his body, his manner.

"You look well," he says. "It's been a while. How are you doing?"

I'm fine, I say. I'm not sure if Hen heard you come in. She's upstairs.

"So she is here?"

She is, I say.

"No need to call her down. This will give us a chance to catch up."

We stand there, awkwardly, barely inside the door.

"What's been going on?"

Work. The house. Life, I say. We're good.

"Glad to hear it. And you're feeling well?"

Yeah, I'm fine. Can't complain.

"That's good," he says. "Very good. Encouraging. And how's our wee Henrietta?"

His casual use of *our* and *wee* in relation to Hen makes me internally wince. As if he knows her. He doesn't know her. He doesn't know us. We aren't his friends.

She's fine, I say, maintaining a blank expression.

I don't tell him how rattled she was after his last visit. How reticent she became, how she treated me for weeks. How long it took for her to return to normal. Sure, that was a long time ago, but I don't want the same thing to happen this time. I don't tell him that I've developed a kernel of animosity toward him because of this, because of the way he made Hen feel. I examine his face again. Those small eyes. Thin lips. He's too pleased to be here, too satisfied and assured. I don't care for it. There's something disingenuous about him, an air of secrecy.

"So it's been a long time. Have you been thinking about me?" he asks, then laughs. "Sorry, I just mean it was a significant visit last time, big news. Sometimes even good news can prime you psychosomatically. It can play havoc with people mentally. I hope things have been stable."

No, I think, things were not stable, not for a while.

We've had things to do, I say. We have lives to live. We can't just sit around and worry about a future that might never happen.

"I understand," he says. "That's good. That's the correct approach. So you'd say the last while has been normal for you guys? You're not feeling anxious? Nothing out of the ordinary? No big fights or issues?"

Hen! I call over my shoulder.

I've decided she should hear this, too.

Hen! I call louder.

She doesn't answer. Maybe she already knows. Maybe she doesn't want to come down and face this man again. Maybe she's up there listening to us, dreading it. I hear her light footsteps upstairs above our heads.

"Yes," she says, from the top of the stairs.

Come here, I say.

She comes down the stairs, slowly. Once she's at the bottom, she sees Terrance and offers a small nod.

"Nice to see you again, Henrietta," he says.

"Hello, Terrance," she replies.

Her voice sounds instantly weary.

"I've just been hearing from Junior about how you guys have been doing. It sounds like things are . . . going well."

She moves in beside me, putting her arms around me. It's rare for her to do this, to be the first to reach out physically. I'm so surprised that I have to stop myself from flinching.

"Yes," she says. "We've been good."

"Shall we sit?" he says. "I have news."

N o need to direct him this time. Terrance clearly remembers the way. We all walk, Terrance leading, into the living room. We sit in the same spots as we did on his first visit—Terrance on the couch, and Hen and I in our chairs close together, across from him. Years have gone by, but what has changed? Very little here, in the house. Everything is the same.

"I'm delighted and relieved," he says, "Overjoyed, really, that you're both keeping—"

Tell us, I say, cutting him off. Tell us the news. That's why you're here.

Hen is calm. She doesn't react to my voice. She doesn't even look up.

Terrance smiles. "Of course." He pauses, sits up straighter. "Junior has made the short list." He waits for this to sink in. He wants it to appear natural, but I'm sure that's part of his protocol, that he's instructed to include these dramatic pauses when he shares the news. He looks at me expectantly. Then to Hen, with a different look, one I can't interpret. "I'm thrilled," he says. "I couldn't *be* more excited. You're another significant step closer to going to space!"

Hen and I look at each other. She brings her hands up to her head, runs them through her hair. She doesn't look startled but drained.

"So he's going for sure?" she asks.

"No, not necessarily," he says. "But he's on the short list, so the chances are much greater now."

Hen puts her hand on mine. Again—unusual. It must be for his benefit.

"What are the timelines?" she asks.

"Let's not get ahead of ourselves," Terrance says. "Nothing's guaranteed, but the ultimate fantasy is closer to becoming a reality."

Whose ultimate fantasy? I wonder.

But then, this doesn't really change anything for us, does it? I say. It's like before: we're still in limbo.

"Yes. I know that might be distressing. I get it. The future is not concrete one way or the other, but I think making the short list does change things," he says. "We have progressed in the right direction. I feel bad for those others who didn't make it. Going forward, we, the three of us, have to focus on the facts, on what's real, not on hypotheticals. This is a significant development. We have a lot to discuss. This visit will be a bit more extensive than the last. It's normal, of course, to have questions. We'll get to that."

I've lowered my head. I'm rubbing my closed eyes. I feel Hen's hand squeeze my leg.

"Guys, come on! This is exciting!" Terrance says. "We have a mandate, a plan for moving forward with everyone on this list. I can assure you, we're not just making this up as we go."

How are we not supposed to think about hypotheticals? I mean, why tell us? I ask. When there's still only a chance of this happening. We don't know anything for sure. So what's the point?

He raises his hands, defensively, nodding his head.

"No, I get it. I do. Really. I know the time between now and my last visit must have felt . . . unusual."

He directs this last word to Hen.

"But I have a question for you," he says. "And it's something I'd like you both to think about: Do you want to live normal, mundane, average lives? Is that really your ambition?"

Hen sits up, listening closer to what he's saying.

"Do you want to be indistinguishable from everyone else? Or do you want to be part of something special and unique? And that, more than anything, is what this is about," he says. "A chance to be a better version of yourself."

The focus has clearly shifted to Hen. It's like all of a sudden I'm not even in the room.

"You can make it all sound pretty good, Terrance," Hen says. "A *better version of yourself.*"

We haven't asked for any of this, I say.

"No, you're right, you haven't. You've been presented with a rare opportunity that, at the moment, remains unresolved. But why is the unknown a burden? It doesn't have to be. It can just as easily be the opposite—a kind of awakening to feel something. I don't just mean the Installation. Even before that. This is a chance to be taken out of your daily, weekly, monthly, yearly routine, regardless of the final outcome. Again . . ." He looks at Hen. Why, why is he fixating so much on her? "This is for both you. It's a chance to wake up. How many people live day to day in a kind of haze, moving from one thing to the next without ever feeling anything? Being busy without ever being absorbed or excited or renewed? Most people don't ever think about the full range of achievable existence; they just don't. This is something we've been working on at OuterMore. You could say it's a company philosophy. Our moral grounding. It's the idea that a true, righteous existence is always achievable, for anyone."

Existence is achievable? I say.

"Existence is achievable! Yes, Junior. You shape your existence through decisions, perceptions, and behavior. It's our company philosophy at OuterMore. Habitual, comfortable activity is the worst kind of prison, because the bars are concealed. You can never learn anything that way. We want people to learn things, not just about new environments but about themselves. Maintaining the status quo is not what being a modern human should be about. This is bigger than the Installation. Do you see what I'm saying? This is what I'm offering you both. An awakening."

"Is this what they tell you to say?" Hen asks. "Because you may as well save your breath."

I can tell she means it. Hen's not one to be resistant by nature. She's not happy about any of this.

"No one tells me what to say. Know that I've been thinking about all of this for a lot longer than you guys. I like you. Both of you. I really do. I want you both to feel in control. I just think you're looking at this the wrong way. And I'm trying to help. That's my job. This has been my life longer than you've been aware of it. It's not just a job but an obsession, a mission I believe in wholeheartedly."

This doesn't affect you, though, does it? I say. Not like it does us. We're the ones in the fishbowl.

Hen turns to me, surprised by my comment, her eyes searching mine.

"It doesn't affect me in the same way, no, of course not. But this venture . . . it's just as big a part of my life as it is yours. This will define my whole career. You're in the fishbowl, yes. But so am I! We're in it together."

"So what happens next?" Hen asks. "Do we get to know anything else today? Are you going to give us anything else?"

Gone is the nervous energy I felt during Terrance's first visit, an energy that stayed in the house for weeks after. Hen's body language— hunched shoulders and feet crossed at the ankles, look to me this time like acceptance.

"I'm going to have to talk with both of you, extensively. There are a series of steps that we'll have to get through."

Steps? What kind of steps? I ask.

"Think of them as interviews," Terrance says. "These will help us, and you, prepare for all potential outcomes."

"When?" Hen demands.

"We'll start tomorrow," Terrance says. "I don't want to inundate you tonight. Just getting the good news is enough for one day. I will maybe trouble you for a glass of water before I leave, though, if that's okay?"

Hen and I look at each other. She stands up and walks out of the room.

Once she's gone, Terrance takes his screen out of his case. He starts taking notes, or writing a message to someone. Then he holds his screen up, aiming it at various parts of the room.

He's taking photos. I'm sure that's what he's doing.

"Don't mind me," he says. "I'm just collecting some data. Don't worry. It's all part of the process. Can you look at me for a second?"

I look at him square in the face. He aims his screen at me.

Click.

It happens before I can stop him.

"Thank you," he says. "Now, before she gets back, I have a few quick questions. You know, like, man-to-man. What has Hen told you, Junior? Be honest. It's in all of our best interests if you tell me the truth."

What does he mean? I have no idea what he's implying. Hen and I don't keep secrets from each other.

Told me? Told me about what? I ask. What do you mean?

Before I can say anything else, Hen returns with his water and sets it down in front of him.

"Ah, yes, great," he says. "Thank you, Henrietta. I remember how good and cold your well water is from last time."

He drinks the entire glass of water, all of it, in one go.

"I can't help but wonder," he says, then turns to me. "I can't help but wonder, Junior, if you ever think back to your life before."

Before what? I ask.

"Before Hen," he says.

B efore Hen. Before Hen.

    What came before is hard to remember. Not that I want to. Those times don't matter.

Now is what's important, not then. Hen is what's important. She's my focus, my everything. My youth was unremarkable, unmemorable. We all occupy a social district, and I had my place: middling, undistinguished, irrelevant. I was the physical embodiment of the numerical mean.

I've always known that, but it's only been recently that I realize whenever I think about the past, I feel a heightened sense of oblivion. I can't go back. I can't. I can't think about those years at all. I can only go forward. I endured the passage of lonely days indifferently. Hen changed that. She gave me a purpose. A reason to exist.

I refuse to be pulled back. I don't have to. I don't have to remember just because Terrance asked me to. I'm not his pet, his toy. There's nothing in those years before that I wish to think about or dwell on. We get only so much mental space in which to store our memories, and there's no reason for me to waste it on what came before. I wasn't myself then. I was someone else, something less, a lesser version of the man I have since become.

Despair is never satisfied on its own. Despair does not want to be alone. Despair wants company. But I feel no despair. Not now. Not going forward.

There really isn't any one memory that sticks out from back then, before Hen. Everything blends into a nebulous fog.

I suppose for someone like me, it's easier to forget.

I t's his loud knocking on the door—*rat tat tat tat tat*—that wakes us. I hear it first, before Hen. I sit up in bed. Confused, initially. Then the knocking becomes light, gentle. Terrance left us sitting in the living room last night. We didn't even walk him to the door. I look over at Hen. She's sprawled out on her stomach. We're naked under one thin sheet. She sighs and opens her eyes.

"What time is it?" she asks, her cheek still resting on the mattress.

I've always thought Hen's at her most striking in these moments, fresh out of the shower, sitting with a full stomach at the table after dinner, first thing in the morning with messy hair and puffy eyes. I think it again this morning as I watch her come to.

"It's still dark," she says. "Shit. He doesn't even let us have coffee first."

Another soft knock on the door. There's nothing aggressive or urgent about this knocking now, which is not the way it started. It's barely perceptible.

Yeah, it's got to be him, I say. Did he say he'd be back this early?

"I don't think so. But, you know."

She rolls over onto her back, brings her hands up to her face, rubbing those swollen eyes.

I'll get it, I say.

I get up, put on my underwear, my shorts. I get to the front door as he's knocking again.

"Did I wake you?" he asks.

You did. What time is it?

"Five thirty," he says. "We have a lot to do today. That's why I gave you the heads-up."

I don't remember the heads-up. He never mentioned a specific time. It doesn't matter now. We're up. He's here.

Come in, I say.

This time, I take him into the kitchen. I show him a seat and turn on the light over the table. This man knows us well, knows things about our life, but until right now, he's only ever seen our front porch, our bathroom, and our living room.

Hen'll be down in a minute, I say. Coffee?

"I'll be fine with some water," he says.

Hen walks in as I'm filling his glass at the sink. She's wearing her usual shorts and black tank top. She walks behind me, over to the coffeemaker. She spoons the grounds into the filter. She coughs a few times, clears her throat.

"Good morning," says Terrance.

"Hey," she says.

I tell them I'll be right back and go to the bathroom to wash my face and brush my teeth. I stand a few steps down the hall and listen, hoping to hear what they say, what they talk about. But, surprisingly, they don't say anything to each other. Nothing at all.

When I return to the kitchen, the percolating coffee is flowing into the carafe. Hen's sitting at the table with an empty expression on her face, a mug waiting in front of her. She has wrapped a strand of hair around her index finger.

"Actually, Junior," Terrance says, "I've started talking with Henrietta. Would it be okay if we keep going? On our own. Then we can have our chat after."

But they haven't been talking. I would have heard them if they had.

You want to talk alone? I ask.

"Yes, that's best."

Hen nods her consent.

Okay, I say. I'll just get a coffee, then I'll go.

We wait silently for the coffee to finish brewing. When the machine starts to hiss, and the pot is full, I still make no motion to leave. I wonder why he wants to do this separately.

"We'll need only about fifteen minutes," Terrance says.

I fill my mug, and Hen's, and return the pot to the warmer.

I'll be out in the barn, I say.

The day we were married is a major moment of reflection for me. It must be for every married couple. Hen and I got engaged three weeks and a day after the first time we talked. It was only a couple of months after I'd seen her for the first time. We were married in the fall, outside. It's another memory I've been thinking about a lot. It was warmer than it was supposed to be for that time of year. I took off my jacket. I rolled up my sleeves above my elbows. Hen wore her favorite dress. It was a soft cotton and had red vertical stripes that made her look like a piece of peppermint candy.

The ceremony itself took no more than ten minutes. Ten minutes, and then Hen got to start over. I did, too. A new start together. She said she could finally put her past behind her, for good. I'd already done that. It was easier for me.

We stood, holding hands. I didn't want to let go. We kissed when we were told to, and then it was official. We were husband and wife and would be together forever. A team of two, till death do us part. For the first time, I could see a desirable future, and it not only excited me but also comforted me. What was real and certain was what I wanted, what I had, right there in front of me.

To new beginnings, I said to Hen. A fresh start.

Hen kissed me again, and I recall her eyes filling with tears. Tears of joy and love.

I 've left them inside to talk. About what, I'm not entirely sure. I usually enjoy my time alone in our old barn. It's true: I don't want Hen to feel neglected, but I do like the extra seclusion out here, how I experience time on my own. Today it feels like I've been ordered out here.

In the barn, I share the space with the chickens only, and they are noninquisitive. They are easy to please. Five minutes, or ten, or thirty, or even hours. It all feels the same out here in the barn. I give the chickens kitchen scraps and water, some grain, and they're always happy to see me. Or if they're not, at least they're impartial. I don't even mind the smell anymore. I'm used to it. Out here, I can be me, and, most important, I can think.

I fill their grain bin. I watch some of the hens digging around. The chickens like to spread out and explore every inch of the barn. Some go at the grain immediately. Others ignore it and continue their erratic scratching of the ground with their claws, periodically tilting their heads and looking up at me. Every so often they unearth a little bug, which they quickly consume.

I rest the grain bag against the wall and walk over to the only window in the barn. It's tiny and covered in dirt and dust. There's a crack in the top-left corner. I spit on it, wipe at it, which does little to increase the visibility. From here I can stake out the house. I can see out of the barn and into the kitchen of my home. I can see Terrance seated at the table. Where's Hen? Maybe they've already had their talk and she's left. He's not talking. A chicken brushes up against my leg. I look down, give a gentle tap with my foot. It shuffles off toward the others.

When I look back at the house, I see her. There she is. She's standing now. She's still in the kitchen. She's just been out of my view. She's up, pacing back and forth. She's speaking ardently, using her hands, gesturing. She's much more animated than usual. Terrance is just sitting there. He might be taking notes on his screen, I can't tell. I think they're arguing. I know Hen. I know her gestures and body language. This appears heated.

I'm surprised. All the time I've seen them together, Hen has barely spoken to Terrance. I'm taken aback that she feels comfortable talking to him—a stranger—the way she is. What could she possibly have to say? Has she been holding it all until she could get him alone? What's gotten her so riled up? She's pointing at him, pointing at Terrance, a man she's met only twice. A man she barely knows. He's motioning for her to sit down. She doesn't. She's still standing, saying something to him. She hasn't let up.

I continue watching until Hen walks away, out of the kitchen. Whatever has upset her, whatever they were talking about, it was intense. Intense, and unresolved.

B ack inside, I find Terrance sitting at the kitchen table. He's alone. No sign of Hen.

"Perfect timing, Junior," Terrance says, "Hen and I literally just finished."

Everything okay? I ask, even though I know it isn't. I saw. Everything is not okay.

"Yes, of course. Why do you ask?"

I don't tell him I was watching from the tiny barn window, that I could see into the kitchen, that I understand Hen, that it's my job to know her, pick up on her signals.

What were you guys talking about?

He's doing something with his screen and is still looking at it as he replies. "We were covering a few general things, nothing much."

Really? I say. Do you know Hen?

"I know her, sure, like I know you, Junior," he says, putting down his screen and looking at me.

How does he know me? Not well. Not at all.

"Now, come here for a second," he says, standing up. "Have a seat right here, yes. That's it, thank you. Have you ever had a custom suit made? Just pretend that's what's happening now, okay? Relax. You seem a bit tense."

I'm not tense, I say. I'm just not used to this. What are you doing?

Terrance is holding his screen up to me.

"Taking some measurements."

Measurements? What for? I thought we were supposed to be talking. That you wanted to get to know me better.

"That's what I'm doing. We can do both. I can take measurements and get to know you better at the same time. This is for the databank. Now that you're on the short list, we need to gather some info."

Did you do this with Hen? I ask.

"No, no, this is just for you. Hen and I chatted," he says casually. "She's really great. You're a lucky guy. Yeah, just hold your arm like that, right there."

This is unusual, uncomfortable even, but I don't see the point in protesting. I need to be patient. To think and to wait for the right moment.

"How are things at work?"

Fine, I say. It's work. Nothing much changes there.

"I get the sense this area is in a bit of a decline. I don't mean that as an insult, just a reality. I know how much the city has grown over the last few decades, at the expense of the rural areas and smaller towns. A lot of people in the city forget there are still folks living all the way out here."

Yeah, well, lots of people have moved away over the years. There aren't many of us left. It's tough around here. Not as many jobs. The isolation can get to people. Some people.

"And yet you both stay here. You and Hen. Is that a choice?"

Nothing's forced, if that's what you mean, I say. It's what we know. We have all we need here. Hen's happy with what she knows. She wouldn't like living anywhere else.

"You're some of the fortunate ones then."

I nod.

"So you do feel like you're making a choice, though, right? That it's your choice to stay all the way out here with Hen?"

I'm not sure what he's getting at. What kind of question is this?

Again, I nod.

"This is important. It's all connected to what we're working on at OuterMore. I don't think people realize that. They think we're motivated only by money and profit. But we're interested in people and community and progression and free will. That's our obsession, and how people can adapt and coexist in a healthy way."

But companies do have an obsession with money, I say. They have to.

"No, not necessarily. It's about movement. It's about adaptability. It's about advancement and stretching the limits of human possibility. It's important to remember the opposite is also possible. Human potential can also shrink and regress."

That's nice to say, but I don't quite believe it. I see it at my work. Everything in some way or another, I say, if it's going to happen, is about money.

"Intention really *does* matter," he says. "Now hold your head back a bit more. Like this."

He moves behind me.

What are you doing? Is this part of the interview?

"Not the formal part, but yes, it is. While we talk, the computer here is acquiring data, like how much CO_2 you exude. How often do you get your hair cut?"

My hair cut? A few times a year.

"Where do you go?"

Where do I go? You mean, who cuts it? I do it myself. Or Hen does. Where is Hen? What's she doing? Is she upset about something?

I can feel his screen making contact with me, touching the base of my neck underneath my hairline. It's warm, hot even.

"Sorry," he says. "This won't take a moment."

How many others have there been?

"Sorry? What do you mean?"

How many others have you met with like this? Like, gone into their homes and collected data.

"Unfortunately, I'm not permitted to talk about anyone else. It's off-limits. And for good reason. I wouldn't feel comfortable telling anyone else about you, either. It's a matter of privacy, which I'm sure you understand. Have you and Hen ever lived anywhere else?"

I hate this question. It bothers me.

This is the only house we've lived in, I answer.

"Does it ever get too quiet for you? For her?"

No, I say. I've told you that we like the quiet, the solitude.

"You never feel lonely?"

I consider the question.

No, I say. I'm not the type to get lonely.

I hear him key something into his screen.

"Okay. But if you're selected, it'll be different for you. You'll be living among others. It'll be close quarters, for a while anyway. That might be tough for you. But at least all the living quarters are climate-controlled."

But I won't have any choice, will I? Like right now, sitting here as you take your measurements. There's nothing I can do about it. So it is what it is.

The screen is moved up, slowly from my neck to the back of my head. I can hear it and feel it processing. Terrance walks around in front of me. He's being careful, thorough.

"Can you hold your feet up?"

My feet?

"Yeah, it'll just take a second."

You mean like this?

I bring my feet up.

I won't have any choice, will I? I say.

"Actually, if you could please hold your legs out straight. It gets a better read. Here, rest it on this."

I put my feet on the chair he's moved into position.

This seems excessive, I say. I don't understand.

"Perfect."

What's this for?

"To get the measurements of your soles."

Why do you need measurements from the bottom of my feet?

"Protocol. Nothing is trivial. It's all part of the process."

I wonder how you'd like it if this was reversed, I say.

He stops what he's doing, looks at me.

"I understand, Junior. I do. This is a lot to take in. It's not ideal, but it could also be a whole lot worse."

Easy for you to say.

"No, it could. Think if we just showed up here with a van, tied you up, threw you in the back, and drove you away."

I don't say anything because I don't know how to respond.

He takes a step back, smiles. "We wouldn't do that. But you know, I'm just trying to give you some perspective."

There's never really any perspective, I say, feeling my agitation growing. It's not an option. Not in the moment. That only happens later. Can I put my feet down?

"Yes, you're good. Thanks. I'd like to keep talking now, if that's okay."

I'd rather not. I'd rather have some time alone, some time to check on Hen.

I'm going to have some more coffee, I say.

"Fine, that's fine. Just do as you normally would."

I fill my mug and sit back at the table. Terrance takes a seat across from me. He puts his screen down between us, rests his elbows on the table, brings his hands together, rubbing them.

"So . . . your house. Tell me about it. What kind of shape was it in when you moved here?"

When we first got it?

"Yeah."

Not great. We knew that. We knew it would be a lot of work to make it livable. That didn't matter. You see what it's like now, and it was in much worse condition. We cleaned and painted.

"Are you good with that kind of work? Repairs, fixing, building?"

Yeah, I can do all that. I did a lot of that. It's still not finished. It's ongoing, constant.

"You moved in right away?"

After we were married, yes.

"Was it empty?"

Mostly. We're still finding stuff every now and then, in the basement and attic.

A strange question. Aren't most houses you move into empty? How did he know ours wasn't?

"In an old house like this I'm sure there are always surprises.

What do you remember from those days? When you two were first living here."

I remember we were happy, I say. Happy to have our own house.

"Can you recall anything specific, like a detail, or is it more a feeling you remember?"

Anybody can remember details if you ask them to, I say, but it doesn't mean it actually *happened* that way.

I wait for him to make eye contact, which he does.

"You have a point, Junior," he says. "You're right."

After Terrance and I finish talking, he follows me around outside like a puppy as I do some chores. He reiterates to behave "according to my custom." He just wants to watch. How am I supposed to behave according to my custom when a virtual stranger is at my house, watching me, observing my every move, taking notes?

But I try. I behave normally. I have some grass to cut and some weeds to pull. He watches my banal routine with sincere curiosity and interest. He makes one call on his screen and walks away from the house, halfway down the lane, to chat in private. At the end of the day, we stand on the porch, Hen and me, as he gets in his car to leave. He tells us not to worry, that he will be in touch at some point.

"Hopefully it will be with good news," he says.

He took so many photos, measurements, and notes, and nothing was ever fully explained. It's an odd feeling to know you might be leaving for a long time, going somewhere that's nearly incomprehensible.

But I think what sticks in my mind even more is his interaction with Hen, what I saw from the barn. Neither of them mentioned it to me. They both assume I'm unaware.

Hen makes stew for dinner. I listen to her cutting the onion and searing the meat. We eat it outside.

Instead of relief, there's a feeling of emptiness since he left, as if our tight bond has been stretched and no longer fits right. I want it to be like it was before he showed up, but as I move a hunk of meat around in the gravy, I realize that will be impossible. We're past that point. I'm not hungry. He's gone, but I can feel his presence, his eyes, as if he were still here watching me. Hen, like me, has barely touched her food.

What did you think of that? I ask.

She doesn't respond. She's making a paste with a mashed piece of diced carrot and gravy.

Hen?

"Yes? What?"

Aren't you going to say anything? If you're upset, you can tell me. I don't know why you would be. But we can talk.

"I'm not upset. I'm sitting here quietly. It doesn't mean I'm upset. Being quiet can mean a lot of things. In this case, it means I'm thinking."

But don't you think that—

"Can't we just eat one dinner without dissecting everything? Without so many questions?"

Is that really a good idea?

"Sometimes I think you can only understand what's happening in front of you this minute. I can't just forget how things used to be, even if it's different now. It hasn't always been easy for us, can't you acknowledge that?"

She stands and carries her bowl inside.

T hree restless nights have gone by, and I'm still fixated on Terrance's visit. I'm thinking about it, about him, too much. I have to just put it out of my mind. Forget about Terrance and OuterMore and the Installation. It's mind over matter.

For now, it's working. I'm getting better at applying my focus elsewhere. I don't think Hen's been as fortunate. She apologized after leaving dinner in such a huff, but it didn't feel entirely sincere. I still said it was okay. Hen has a difficult time controlling her emotions. I've tried to ask her about it, but she gives me a one- or two-word answer and then deflects the topic.

That's why it's Hen I'm worried about, not me. I've reassured her that I'm not bothered. I try to help her, do whatever I can to alleviate her unease.

I've been noticing new things about her since Terrance's last visit. Subtle stuff. She doesn't seem herself. Something's off. Last night I came into our room before bed and saw her standing at the window. She didn't hear me, didn't know I was there. She wasn't doing anything. Her back was to me. She was staring outside, one hand against the window frame. We must have stood like that—me looking at her, her looking out the window—for more than a minute before I took another step, which she heard because the floor creaked and she turned around.

She walked over to me, took my hand, led me to bed. She took off my clothes, got on top of me. We had sex. It didn't last long. When it was over she rolled off me and moved to her side of the bed without a word. She kept the sheet off her. She fell asleep. I didn't. I stayed awake.

Good news for someone often means bad news for someone else. I wonder if the others on the short list are experiencing a similar domestic agitation, a ruffling of the feathers of routine. How many others are there? Where do they live? There's so much Terrance hasn't told us. There were so many questions I had, ones I'd prepared over the course of two long years, but then when he was there in front of me, my mind went blank.

If Hen's worried about my leaving, I get it. I would understand that, if she'd say it. I just want her to be honest with me. Open. To talk. To explain how she feels. Because I'm not good at this. I can't guess. And we need to do this together, to get through this together, not separately.

I know she's quiet by nature, reserved, understated. But if she told me more, opened up, I could help her. I'm sure of it.

It's because of Hen that we have a house at all. I give her all the credit. She found the place. We used to talk more, when things were still new between us. When we were still eager to learn about each other. That's what that time was about. It was about talking and listening, learning about the other—interacting, observing, experiencing. It takes time. I've been trying to remember these earlier moments more, reflect on them, focus on them.

It was Hen who convinced me to take the job at the feed mill, and I'm still working there, all these years later. I remember it well. She didn't tell me to do it. We talked about it not long after getting together. If she'd just told me to do it, to take the job, who knows, maybe I wouldn't have done it. An order might have turned me off. I told her how I'd met Mr. Flowers, the owner of the mill, how he'd offered me the job. We discussed the timing and if it was the right job for me.

"It sounds pretty good. It's steady work, physical, and the mill's not going anywhere. The money's okay. There doesn't seem to be much downside."

We were lying outside in the grass, in the shade, where it was coolest.

Yeah, I said.

We were both on our backs, hands behind our heads, looking straight up, only our feet touching.

We would talk about many different things, but often about the future, where we'd be years down the road. We preferred what hadn't happened yet to what had.

"You need to work. But people have to make up their own minds," she said. "When they don't, it doesn't always end well. This has to be your choice to make, not mine."

This is how we used to talk. Back and forth. Open. Interested. Supportive.

What would you do if you were me? I asked.

"I would take the job. It's fair pay for honest work. It's good experience. But it doesn't matter what I would do. I'm not the one doing the job. Try answering this: What do you want?"

What do I want from what? I asked.

"I'll say it again. Think about it: what do you want?"

That's when I kissed her. She closed her eyes as I did it. I can still picture it whenever I want to, replaying it in my mind, over and over. That's a detail I could tell Terrance about. If I wanted to. But I don't want to.

I owe what I have now—my job, my house, my life—to my wife. All of it. I am who I am because of Hen. I have to keep that in mind. I can never forget that. She can be erratic at times, frustrating, unpredictable, and, recently, standoffish. But she's supported me through everything. That's what a relationship is for: mutual support and acceptance. No one understands me the way she does. And that means something.

To me, it means everything.

Another sleepless night. For me, anyway. I suppose it's understandable. Hen's already awake when I open my eyes. She's on her side, looking at me. It's been more than a week since we last saw Terrance.

"It's supposed to be hotter than yesterday," she says. "Does it bother you? Do you find it affects your sleep or how you feel?"

You mean the heat? I ask.

"Yeah."

I roll over, swing my feet out, and stand up. I stretch, cough twice, and clear my throat. I'm glad she's talking, asking questions. It's refreshing. It's like old times.

I guess I feel it, I say. Like you, I'm aware of it, but I'm also used to it. It's always hot around here. It doesn't bother me much. The more you think about it, the worse it is.

"Do you like it here?"

I turn back to her. She's still looking at me.

Of course. This is my home.

"I know, I know. But do you feel *happy* here?"

Why would you ask that, Hen? Yes, I'm happy here. Are you?

"Junior, would you do anything for me?"

What? I ask.

If she didn't completely have it before, she definitely has my full attention now.

"Do people ever actually question why they get married in the first place? What do I mean to you? Us. What am I to you?"

You're my wife. We have a life together. Maybe I don't understand what you're asking.

"Tell me about our wedding day."

This question. This question, of all she could have asked, she asks this one. It puts me at ease. It's like a release valve. I know how to answer this. The memory is so clear.

It was a great day, I say, sitting back down on the bed. I think about it often. I could tell you everything about it.

Hen doesn't comment on anything I've just said. Instead, she looks at me. It's me who breaks the eye contact.

"Can I talk to you about anything?" she asks.

Yes, you can.

Hen's never been much of a talker, but I think it's best to encourage her if she has that inclination, especially under the circumstances.

It's about OuterMore and my leaving, I say. Isn't it?

"No, it's not," she says. "I don't want to talk about that. It's about our relationship."

I think our relationship is great, I say.

"No," she says, touching my arm. "I just want to talk, okay? I'm not asking you for answers or solutions to anything. I just need to talk and tell you what I'm feeling."

I don't think this is the best way to have a discussion, but I nod regardless. If she thinks this will help, I should let her try.

"We've been married for seven years. That's not a very long time, but it feels like it. I know it's been different since Terrance showed up two years ago, but I've been thinking more about the years before he showed up. It's not that anything dramatic or drastic has happened between us. You've never hurt me physically; you've never cheated on me. What I mean is, this isn't a particular charge against you or something you've done. I'm thinking about us and how we interact and how we live out here without anyone else around. I wonder about the city sometimes and what it would be like there. I've never been anywhere else. That idea scares me and excites me, and I know you'd never go to the city. I've never said anything to you before because it's hard to bring these things up. But, honestly, it feels good to say it."

She was looking at her hands throughout this whole speech, talking to them, but she looks up now, at me.

I think you'd hate the city, Hen, I say. It's busy and dirty and there are so many people around. This is what you know. It's understandable to wonder from time to time. That's fine, but long-term? You'd hate it. This is where you're from. This is your home.

She waits before she responds. Her expression doesn't give anything away.

"What do you think about more, Junior, the past? Or the future?"

I have to consider her question before I answer. The answer, I believe, is that I think more about the future, but I don't know if that's what she wants to hear.

She sighs. "It's okay. Sorry," she says. "I don't mean to rant or pepper you with questions like this first thing in the morning."

No, it's fine, I say. Don't apologize. You don't have to apologize. You can talk to me whenever. I want you to.

She smiles at me. It is the first time in a while she's smiled warmly at something I've said.

"If you feel like I've been distant recently, that's not what I'm trying to do. It's not your fault. This is just a weird time for me. I'm doing my best. I really am."

I know you are.

"I had no idea what to expect out of this. How could I? This whole thing's bigger than us." She looks at me again. "Who knows when we'll see Terrance next? But when we do, just . . ."

Just what? I ask.

"Nothing. I shouldn't . . . I'm not supposed to . . . I don't *need* to say anything. Terrance is harmless, that's all. I wanted you to know that."

How do you know? How do you know he's harmless?

"It's obvious to me. Forget that. This is supposed to be about us, about our relationship. And we've had our share of issues, but just know that I'm trying."

I don't know how to respond. It's the most open and honest she's been in weeks, maybe even years. I walk over to the window, touching her shoulder as I pass. The barn looks quiet. It's nice to be up this early.

I'll go make some coffee, I say, walking out of the room.

She doesn't respond.

After setting the coffee to brew, I call up to Hen to see if she wants anything else while I'm down here. I wait, but again, she doesn't reply. It's possible she went back to bed and fell asleep. I pop a couple of slices of bread into the toaster. Hen likes her coffee black and her toast bone-dry. Not even butter. She's happy to eat it cold, too.

I carry her toast and a mug of coffee upstairs.

Here, I say, stepping back into the room. I'll leave this. For whenever you're ready for it.

"Thanks," she says.

I walk out, go down the hall to the bathroom. Turn on the tap. I didn't have to bring her breakfast in bed. It was a nice thing to do. A thoughtful gesture. I'm splashing handfuls of cold water onto my face when I hear her yell.

"Junior!"

What is it? I call.

I run to the room. She's standing at the window. The plate with her toast is on the dresser, untouched.

"Look," she says.

I don't have to look to know. He's back. He's returned.

"He wasn't supposed to be back yet, not so soon," she says, but not really to me.

She throws on a shirt and we walk downstairs together, me behind her. We wait at the door. I'm staring at the floor. We hear the car door close, his steps coming up onto the porch. We wait for the knock.

Rat tat tat tat tat.

Terrance, in his suit, is smiling when Hen opens the door. He has his case but also a large suitcase on wheels beside him. He's never had that before. He wipes a small, polka-dot hanky along his brow.

Tell us, I say. Tell us why you're here.

"You've been selected, Junior. You've been chosen. You'll be going away. You're going to be part of the Installation."

W e're back in the living room. Terrance has his screen out, but he isn't taking notes—he's recording. Hen is sitting there, looking down at her hands. It's a pose that's become familiar to me, and dreaded. My heart rate has picked up, that's for sure.

Do you need to record this? I ask.

"Unfortunately, yes. It's policy."

I don't know what you want to hear from me, I say. I can't say I was hoping for this.

"The whole point of this isn't to pick people who are the easiest to take or who most want to go. That's not how we complete the lottery. It has to be random. How could we decide between someone with a child and someone, say, with an elderly parent in need? Whoever gets selected can rest assured that anyone left at home will be well provided for and taken care of."

I don't get that. I don't see why it wouldn't be better to send the people who want to go, I say.

"Junior, come on, we've talked about this. You have to trust us. There'd be way too many volunteers. To get the best understanding of the effects of life there, we need the group to be as random as possible. It's not realistic to assume that in the next wave, when the move is permanent, that everyone's going to want to go. They won't be coming back. This is about research and understanding. Do you know about conscription during the old wars? If you got picked, you had to go. And that was to war. Not to be part of something positive, something astonishing and progressive, like this."

This is crazy, I say. It doesn't feel right to me.

I feel like they should be sending others, someone else. And why is it always Terrance coming here alone?

He turns away from me. "How have you been feeling, Henrietta?"

"Fine," she says, looking up for the first time, locking eyes with him. "Just fine."

"You don't seem overly surprised by the news."

There's a cool steadiness to his voice, a calmness. I don't like it.

"You're right, Terrance, I'm not overly surprised."

"This is going to be a good thing. You'll see. I'm so happy for you, for both of you. You're part of history. If you have any questions, anything at all, I want to sit here and answer them, as long as it takes. But you also might feel like letting the news settle. So, if there's nothing that you want to know immediately, I'm going to leave you for now. But I'll be back."

"What's with the suitcase?" asks Hen quickly. "You've never had that before."

I see now how tired she looks, her eyes are ringed and heavy.

"Well, as I said, I'm leaving. But I'll be back, and I'll be staying for a bit."

Here? I ask.

"Yes. I know this sounds like an imposition, but given our situation, it's absolutely necessary. If you recall, on my first visit, it was explained in the paperwork—that I would be back to stay temporarily if Junior was selected."

"I don't remember that," says Hen. "No, I'm sure that was never discussed, not at any point. Why do you have to stay here?"

I don't recall anything about that, either, I say.

"Which is common," he says. "There's always a lot to take in on that first visit. Hard to remember details when you get good news."

"Why do you have stay here, Terrance?" Hen demands.

"Because I do, Henrietta," he answers sharply. Then he readjusts his voice to his normal, overtly friendly timbre. "We're going to be busy bees, working closely together, so I need you to work with me. I'll be back. But first I think the two of you should be alone for a few days. I think you should celebrate! There's no more worrying or wondering about what the future holds. It's official! You're going to be part of something that's very far-reaching and important. It's for real. It's happening."

W hat are you doing? I ask. I know this is stressful, but you've been puttering around alone up there for over an hour.

Hen went upstairs after Terrance left, to the room down the hall, the guest room. I stayed in the living room, listening to her shuffling around, until I decided to go upstairs and investigate.

"I'm trying to sort some of this, get this stuff out of here. I'm thinking almost all of it should be chucked. I hate having this clutter. It's crap. It weighs me down. How have we collected so much stuff? It's not like we've been living here for twenty years. But there's twenty years of shit and baggage."

Not all of it's shit, Hen.

"Pretty much," she says.

Is it so important to clear this room out now? I say. I was hoping to talk to you, about how you feel.

"You were hoping to talk to me about how I feel? Really?"

Yes. You sound surprised.

"It's not like you," she says.

Well, considering the situation, there's a lot to discuss.

"Yes and no," she says. "We're in this now. It's not like talking about it is going to change anything."

Hen, I say, taking another step toward her, I'm worried about you.

Her expression changes, softens a little.

"What are you worried about?"

I worry about leaving you here, about what you'll do while I'm gone.

I don't tell her everything I'm worried about. How I'm concerned what my leaving will mean for us. That it's a long time to be gone. That this is all I've ever known.

"Your face," she says. "It's flushed."

I'm trying to tell you, I say. I don't feel good about this.

"You have nothing to worry about. Trust me."

I don't understand you. You're acting like this isn't a big deal, as if we get this kind of news every day. I'm leaving! Don't you get that?

Now I can *feel* my face flushing. I can feel my blood pumping and moving. It's unpleasant. And her first impulse was to come up here, away from me, in this moment, and start sorting through old stuff. That's what I find most distressing. The more I think about it, the more it upsets me.

"I'm acting like I have to, okay? There's no way to plan for this. I'm reacting and figuring it out as I go. That's all. If you can't understand that, there's nothing I can do."

These are the last few days we'll have alone for a long time, I say. Terrance said we should be celebrating. Enjoying our time together. Shouldn't we at least try to—

"Try to what?"

I don't know, I say. Try to savor our days? We should make the most of it. We have limited time now. Limited time together.

"I have so many questions in my head, questions and concerns and complaints you can't even begin to understand, and I just thought it was better to be busy tonight and feel like I'm being productive rather than wondering what's going to happen next and what the consequences of this, of all of this, are going to be."

What questions do you have? I ask, sitting down on the floor and pulling her next to me. I want to know. I have questions, too.

There are boxes and piles of things scattered around us. She looks so tired, stressed. I put my hand on her knee.

I don't want to argue, I say.

"There was a time when we didn't argue at all," she says. "At the beginning. You wouldn't remember."

I consider this but don't respond.

"And it's not even that I want to clean up. I just want to be busy, at least for now. I don't know. This is all happening faster than I was expecting. What worries me more, though, is that now we hear he's coming to stay. Why couldn't he have told us that earlier?"

I lean over to kiss her. She offers me her cheek, not her lips.

"It's not a usable guest room when it's like this."

I close my eyes, lean away from her.

Terrance isn't my biggest concern, Hen. You are, I say. I don't care if he'll be comfortable in here or if it'll be crowded.

"I've been meaning to clean up for a long time anyway. I feel like if we sit around and talk about things, it won't do anything for me. Nothing changes. Can you see that? No, of course you can't. That's what I'm realizing. Nothing changes, not for me."

That's fine, I say, I know we're different. I know we deal with change differently. But Terrance is not going to care what his room is like. I don't want you stressing over Terrance.

"I'm not stressing over *Terrance*! This whole thing is stressful. My life is stressful, Junior!"

This is his doing. We didn't ask for any of it, I think.

"He'll be staying in here, and I don't even know what half this stuff is. You don't need these."

Her movements are quick and forceful, which confirms she's upset, angry. I stare at the gloves in her hands.

I work so much with my hands, lifting and sorting. Here's proof of that. These old gloves. I wore right through the palm of both after a couple of months' use. I have no idea what prompted me to keep them, to store them away when they are so tattered. Why would I keep them?

"Look, there are holes in the palm and fingers. And they stink."

No, I say. Keep them. They're better when they're worn in. I hate breaking in new gloves.

"You'll never wear these."

You don't know that. I might. Plus, these objects, they remind me of things.

"This is why we have so much stuff. If you think like that, you'll never get rid of anything. It's not healthy. This is a chance to clean up, to clean house, throw stuff out. Don't you see that?"

I don't consider it much of a chance to throw my belongings away, my memories. A chance usually means it's a good thing. If it's in here and not tossed already, there's a reason.

"You know what I mean."

Not really.

"We never come in this room anymore. So many boxes. I have no idea what any of it is."

Are you going to go through it all tonight? It's already getting late.

"No, I don't know. I've started now."

Listen, I don't want you throwing anything out, I say, my voice rising. All of this is mine, and if you just toss it all out, I'll never know what . . . what . . .

I can't finish the thought. I'm at a loss for words, and I don't know why I feel so attached.

I might need these things, okay? I say.

My tone, assertive and sharp, surprises her, I can tell. It surprised me, too. I don't often talk like this.

"What's wrong with you? Why are you getting so worked up?"

Nothing's wrong. I'm not getting worked up.

"You are. You're yelling. You shouldn't be yelling."

I'm not yelling, I just feel a bit blindsided. I don't know why you get like this. Why tonight of all nights.

"You have to calm down. I'm not doing something or trying to start something. All I'm doing is getting rid of clutter and making space. You're the one—"

I thought we were having a quiet, relaxing night together. A celebration. I guess that was wishful thinking. Now I find you all alone up here, doing this. Everything in here has value to me. All of it!

Hen gets up. Her back to me. She pushes aside a box and steps into the closet.

"A quiet night together, ah, *just the like the old days*?"

There's derision in her tone. Derision and indignation.

Pardon me?

"Forget it," she replies, and turns back to her sorting.

So much stuff that just sits in the dark for years. But it's not garbage. It makes up who I am. My memories. To dispose of them because she happens to be in one of her moods—that isn't right.

I've shared years here with Hen. Without substance, how can I maintain an identity? Why does she want to forget? Why does she want to forget us?

I watch her struggle on all fours to move some boxes to the side, to get deeper into the closet. She's already removed several large bins and two shoe boxes from the heap, which are pushed against the wall. The room has become almost entirely dark in the fading light. Hen has grabbed a headlight. She turns it on but doesn't wear it. She's bent over, hidden deep in the back of the closet.

"AHHHH!" she yelps, and then jumps out from the closet, her eyes shut.

"Did you see that?" she says. "That. In there."

I take her headlight and step into the closet. I shine the light into the corner. I see it there, in the spot beside an old shirt. It's in the beam of light, not moving.

I keep the light on it, bend down for a closer look. I find it . . . enthralling. Unfamiliar.

Shit, I say. That is weird. I've never seen one like it.

"It's so big," she says. "They keep getting bigger. I thought they eradicated them years ago, got rid of them all in the area."

Did they? I don't know, I say. I don't remember.

It's not doing anything. Nothing at all. I want to keep looking at it. The desire is strong. It's almost hypnotic. Its long, thin tentacles are twitching. It doesn't appear scared or nervous, but calm, knowing, poised, ready.

"Just what we need," she says. "An infestation. They'll get into the walls. They must be coming inside from the canola fields."

It's not an infestation, I say. It's only one.

"One is too many," she says.

Why isn't it moving? I think. Why isn't it scuttling away, hiding?

I can't take my eyes off this large insect. I know nothing about these creatures. Nothing. Not a thing. How can that be? It's living here in my house, living in the same rooms I live in. Yet I never knew.

"I'm definitely checking under the bed for more."

Then, I feel her foot lightly kick my back.

"Junior? You haven't budged. You're staring. What are you doing?"

I'm not sure. But you don't have to worry, I say. I'll take care of it.

"Well, good. Because I don't want to. I'm done in here for tonight. I'm going to bed," she says. "Get that thing outside."

You should rest.

I'm still looking at the beetle when she walks out. Its body is shiny black, with intermittent yellowish stripes. It's impressive, about two inches long. The antennae are about twice as long as the body. It's the three horns that are most dramatic. Two on either side of the head and one in the middle, extruding upward.

It comes to me. A horned rhinoceros beetle. That's it, that's what they're called.

Hen mumbles something at the door, but I don't catch it.

Uh-huh, I say, without turning around. There's nothing to worry about. I'll take care of it.

I woke up before the alarm. I lay there for a while beside Hen. Just the two of us. She wasn't snoring, but I could hear her breathing and know she is dead to the world. Her mouth is open. I lean over and kiss her on the forehead, on the soft spot above her left eyebrow. She closes her mouth, swallows once, but doesn't open her eyes. I get up, head downstairs.

Something about seeing that beetle last night invigorated me, cleared my head, got me out of my narcissistic, self-obsessed neurosis. I couldn't understand anything about it, why it was there, what it was doing. Where had it come from? How was it surviving all alone in that dark closet? How long had it been there? Why wasn't it moving? Why didn't it want to escape? Was it even aware of itself? All of these ambiguities not only transfixed but relaxed me.

I watched it for a while. I don't know how long. Observing it. Then I went to bed.

Although I slept well, I had the sense in the night that Hen was tossing and turning, that she was getting up and down, as if our night roles had been reversed. I have a recollection of seeing her at the window in the middle of the night, looking out at the barn and the back field.

Poor Hen. This has been hard on her. After setting the coffee, I sit with my screen, scrolling through it aimlessly. I eat a piece of cheese from the fridge and turn on the weather forecast. More sun and heat. More humidity. Another day of extreme UV. They're predicting a 40 percent chance of thunderstorms in the evening, like they do every day.

I should go out to the barn, see the chickens and get the chores done. The earlier the better on these sweltering days. I pour Hen a coffee and carry it back upstairs. She's gone from the room. The shower's on. I open the bathroom door and pop my head in.

I'm going to work now, I say. How'd you sleep?

She doesn't answer. She must not hear me over the water. She's probably shampooing her hair. I set her plain black coffee down by the sink.

I'm off to work then, I say.

No answer.

U nlike most days after my shift at the mill, I'm not in a hurry to get home. I should be. It's my last night alone with Hen for a while, for who knows how long. I can't explain it. I'm just not ready to go back yet.

I feel like driving around, without a destination, just driving for the sake of driving, without anyone telling me what to do or where to go, for a change.

Hen always has suggestions for things I should be doing when I'm at home, little jobs that I can tackle if I have a moment. She doesn't like me being idle. I take care of all the repairs around the house, even the ones I don't enjoy doing. It's rare for me not to have some kind of duty or purpose.

I send Hen a message:

Have to stay at work later than I thought. I'll eat when I get home. You don't have to wait.

I don't like to lie, especially not to Hen. I rarely, if ever, do. But this is a small lie, a fib. Insignificant in the grand scheme of things. It's for her own good. If she knew the truth, her feelings might be hurt.

Many of these back roads around here have been left to crack and crumble and disintegrate. It's alarming. There's no money to fix them, I guess, and even if there were, no one would care enough to make it happen. Our roads aren't worn out from overuse but from neglect.

I know Terrance has continued to say that I should be excited, that I should thrilled for this opportunity of a lifetime. But I'm just not. This opportunity is a beginning. I understand that intellectually. So why does it feel like an end?

Maybe it's me. Maybe there's something wrong with me.

On a whim, I stop the truck on the side of the road and get out. The sky is streaked with reddish pink and hazy, thin clouds. The sun is fading but hasn't set yet. It's lovely. I have the bizarre urge to go for a walk, right here in the fields, because I can.

The canola is starting to bloom. The plants are over my head by a foot or so and make me feel like I'm underwater. The yellow gets so bright it's almost fluorescent. There's also a noise in here, nearly imperceptible, but it's there when you're this close. A subdued arthropod buzzing.

I don't think I'm looking for anything. I'm just going farther into the field, the canola flowers brushing up against me. I'm so far in now I can't see the truck anymore. It feels good to be in here, covered and hidden. No one knows where I am. I want to remove my boots, my socks, too, and I do. I carry them in one hand. I like how the dirt feels on my bare feet.

It's getting darker, but I'm not ready to go back yet. Maybe I'm just delaying the inevitable. I continue on, walking slowly, straight ahead, moving aside the plants with my free hand.

I stop periodically to look up at the sky, the twilight. Another day gone. That's when I see it above me, filling the sky to the south. I can smell it now. Smoke.

It's billowing up into a thick cloud. I start to jog, then run. The smoke is everywhere all of sudden, filling the sky. It must be a massive blaze to produce this amount of smoke. There's a barn in this field. That's what must be on fire.

I've been told these old barns are physical reminders of an older life, when things were different. They need upkeep. They need to be restored. It would be a tragedy if the one in this field is ablaze. Another barn lost. I take my shirt off and wrap it around my face as a mask. It's hard to see with all the smoke.

Barn fires have become more common over the last year or so. There is debate about who's setting them on fire. Is it old farmers who want to protest the loss of their land, or is it the canola corporations burning down the remaining barns so they can take over more land? Whoever it is, it's not good. Fires are dangerous around here. They can spread and burn for days.

I spot it up ahead. The barn. It's fully engulfed in flames. The heat is immense. I might be able to help. I might be able to put it out somehow, or at least get it under control until help arrives.

I should have just gone home to Hen and spent the night with her. It was a mistake to come here. This isn't good. But I'm here now. I can't change that. Before this week, I would have turned around and fled. Things are different now. I feel my sense of duty expanding, and this, too, can be my duty. I can't be a bystander. I have to be brave, take control. I have to act. I take a breath and run toward the fire.

Six or seven steps into my run, I'm hit on the back by something, someone. I'm helpless and fall onto my face. My shoulder strikes something hard, a rock. My forehead slams into the ground, the wind knocked clear out of me. I feel the full weight of something fall onto me. Or someone. I gasp for air. I can't move.

What happened? It's a person. A person is here with me? Who? Who did this? Someone must have been following me. The pain is stinging and severe. I taste blood. My lip must be bleeding from hitting the ground. I try to spit, but my face is too close to the ground. There's a knee or elbow in my back, keeping me pinned down. I try to steady my vision but can't. It takes a moment for my eyes to adjust. I pull my head off the ground just enough to see a see a man ahead. Not the one holding me here. A man in a suit, wearing gloves. He's talking to someone else.

"Don't move it," he's saying. "Stay there. Don't let him move."

The person holding me down speaks. "I had to do it," he says. "I had no choice."

"This was for your own good," the man in the suit says, lowering his voice, addressing me this time. "We thought you were going to run into the fire. We couldn't risk losing you."

I've never seen such a violent fire. I try to get up, but I can't. I feel the pressure on my back relent. The person isn't holding me down anymore, but there's too much pain.

"Stay down. Stay where you are."

It's my shoulder. It's both numb and throbbing.

Let me get up, I say, looking into the glare, feeling the heat.

Sweat is dripping into my eyes and falling onto the dry earth. I'm dizzy. I can't see anymore. I close my eyes. I let my head fall down.

"Don't worry," the man in the suit says. "We're here to take care of you."

I wake in a state of terror. A frenzy. My tongue feels heavy and cumbersome. It's difficult to swallow. I can feel my eyes, like an insect's, darting around the room, taking it in. I don't recognize this place or anyone in it.

"Junior? Are you awake?"

I try to get my bearings. It comes to me. This is my home; I know that. I don't know what happened or how I got here, though. I realize the disturbing events from the field weren't a twisted nightmare but reality. My reality. My mouth is so dry. I can't remember much beyond the pain and commotion, the smoke, the man in the suit. The man holding me down. A fire. I can't believe there was actually a fire. A raging fire.

I'm sitting, reclined, in my chair facing the window in the living room. It's Hen. She's standing above me, talking to me. I'm not wearing a shirt. Where's my shirt? There's a fan directed right at me.

Why? Am I hot? I can't quite tell. I try to stand up, but my legs are wobbly.

"No, no, just wait. Stay down."

What happened?

"You had quite the night," Hen says. "You had a lot of people worried."

I can't. I don't remember everything. I can see flashes, but . . . How did I . . . , I start to say.

"Get home? You don't remember?"

No.

"You had an accident. You hurt yourself, but you're going to be fine. I'm going to get you some water."

She leaves me to go to the kitchen. I peer around the room. Something feels different, but I can't tell what, as if Hen has moved a piece of furniture to a different spot. I hear a toilet flush. From upstairs. If Hen's in the kitchen, who's in the bathroom? I thought it was just the two of us. Me and Hen.

"Good morning, Junior. It's good see you up. I came as soon as I heard. My god, you gave us a terrible fright. How are you feeling?" Terrance asks as he walks down the stairs. He stands in front of me, wiping his hands on his pants.

I'm feeling fine, I say. It's not so bad. Just a bit hazy on details.

Terrance steps closer, his smile fading.

"I hope this wasn't done intentionally, Junior. I really hope not. An injury doesn't change anything about the Installation. You know that, right?"

What? You think I . . . Do you think I did this on purpose? I don't even know what happened.

Just as quickly as it faded, his smile returns.

"Good. That's good." He takes a long breath in. "We had our doctor check you out. We were lucky to get him here so fast."

Doctor? A doctor came here?

"Yes, he left about an hour ago. You were still asleep. It's good that you got some rest."

We don't have insurance, you know.

"It's taken care of. You're our responsibility. Your injuries are serious, but you're lucky it's not worse. You won't be able to use that arm for the next while. And you'll have to get used to that recliner of yours."

Why?

"You can't sleep lying down. You can recline to about forty-five degrees, but that's it. How's the pain?"

I can't sleep lying down?

"No, the doctor did a very minor procedure and—"

He did a procedure?

"Yes, on your shoulder, the tendon, and it went very well. He put that dressing on and said to leave it covered. You'll fully recover and be no worse for wear."

I don't really feel it, I say. My shoulder. Not anymore. It's numb, I guess.

"He gave you some meds. You'll have to keep taking them for the next week or so. He left them with me. How are you feeling, Junior? Are you okay?"

I'm thirsty, but otherwise, I feel pretty good.

"I'm happy to hear it. We've got a lot of work to do, you and me."

Hen returns with my glass of water and hands it to me.

"What were you talking about?" she asks.

I look up at her, but she's looking at Terrance.

"I was filling Junior in a bit more," he says. "About his injury."

So it'll get better? I say, after a long, satisfying sip of water. My shoulder?

"It will, not to worry. If you rest and don't overdo it, you'll be back to normal before long."

I don't know how it's going to work down here, in this chair, trying to sleep.

"Who knows? Maybe you'll sleep better down here. It's probably cooler than upstairs."

I'm sorry, but I still don't know why you have to be here right now, I say, trying to sit up but straining under the pain. I appreciate your concern, but before anything else, I need to recover. And this should be a time for Hen and me to be here alone, our last few days together before —

"You've known about the possibility of being picked for a couple of years, Junior. You have had all those days with your wife. All that time to be with her, have quality time with her. But now we have work to do. These will be good days, I promise. This is what you're meant to do."

But I'm seriously injured. You said so yourself. Doesn't that change things at all? Can't we pump the brakes on this a bit?

"I'm afraid that the schedule is fixed."

How are these days supposed to be anything but awkward and stressful? I ask.

"I will disrupt as little as possible. That's the entire aim, in fact. To be unobtrusive. To blend in. And we'll have our time to talk, too. You'll still have lots of time alone. I'm not here to make demands. I'm here to observe."

Observe what?

I feel Hen approach my chair, which makes me feel slightly better.

"We'll discuss everything."

Just tell me what you mean, I say, rubbing my shoulder. What will you be observing?

He runs his tongue over his upper teeth and flashes that smile.

"Same as always," he says. "You."

It's a familiar situation that is making me increasingly uncomfortable. The three of us—Me, Hen, and Terrance—are sitting in the living room. Terrance has promised to explain everything, to tell us in detail why he's here, again, and what's going to happen next. I've demanded it. No more pussyfooting around or making vague references. I'm not in the mood for his hazy explanations.

Terrance seems more excited somehow, on edge. "Junior, you're going to be leaving soon. That's confirmed. We're going to do everything we can to ensure that we get him back to you, Henrietta, safe and sound and ready to carry on your lives together after his life-changing adventure. It's a separation, but a temporary one."

Hen and I look at each other for a beat, then back to Terrance. It's her turn. She needs to step in here. I'm expecting her to ask the obvious question: How long will I be gone? But she doesn't ask. And it bothers me that she doesn't.

Terrance continues his lecture. "The Installation involves a certain amount of risk, but safety and overall well-being: these are our biggest concerns. I can't emphasize this enough. It was decided early on that negligence would be unacceptable. Even more than research or results, taking care of our lottery winners is of utmost importance. You have to believe me, okay? I say this as a friend."

You're not my friend, I think.

That's the least I would expect, I say. That you guarantee my safety. I'm still more worried for Hen than I am for myself.

"Of course, and I'm not just referring to your well-being, Junior. You're the one leaving, but for us, you're both part of this equally. This is a family. This departure affects Hen just as much as it affects you. It's a joint venture. Your communal welfare is an obligation we fully accept and take very seriously."

Right, I say, so what are you getting at?

Hen is picking at one of her nails nervously, a bad sign.

"You'll each have your own set of challenges once you're gone. Henrietta's our responsibility, too."

He turns his attention to Hen, looking at her.

"We're concerned about you, my dear. Not just about your partner here."

"Is that right?" she says.

Terrance coughs into his hand. When he speaks again, it's more pointed, and he's aiming it at Hen as if I'm not here. "Only one family on the short list is given a special resource when their loved one leaves. The lottery was random, but not this part. Hen, you're not alone, right? You've never been alone. And you're not going to be alone."

I feel a flutter in my stomach, followed by an electric twinge in my shoulder. I grab it with the opposite hand.

How long, I say. How long will I be gone?

"Junior is going to be gone for a long time," Terrance says to Hen. "We're talking years, not months. And let's be honest. You guys don't exactly have a huge support system at arm's length. You live in an isolated area. Neither of you has family nearby. We understand what a strain this could be on your marriage. Junior will be facing his own demands on the trip, but so will you, back here, carrying on with life, waiting for him."

Hen's not saying anything. She's just glaring at him.

A thought occurs to me. Maybe I've misunderstood. Is he going to say that she's coming, too? That they've decided it makes more sense for us to go together? The notion sends a warm rush through me. It's a pleasing prospect.

"We've done a lot of investigating and analysis. You won't know the exact date of return, and that makes it harder to carry on. What we don't want is for you to be sitting here, waiting, hoping, all alone, wondering, going crazy. It would be harder on you, than someone in the city, someone with lots of support. You need to keep going on with your life, to try to be as normal as possible."

Hen stops picking at her nail. "Normal? You want me to be normal. Okay. I'll be normal."

Terrance appears oblivious to her backhanded tone.

You want my wife to act normal, I say, after I've been selected abnormally and taken away? Can you hear what she's trying to tell you? There's nothing normal about this situation.

"Of course not, but we will lessen the impact of your departure. And we now have the technological wherewithal to help."

Hen isn't reacting. Why isn't she protesting more? Or asking questions? Is she waiting to hear more, or is she too overwhelmed to say anything? When she's like this—silent, intense, unreadable, closed off—it's hard to know what she's thinking or feeling. I don't like it when she gets like this. She becomes indecipherable. It's unfair. It's childish.

"Being alone, it's a tricky thing. It's good for us, in doses, but not for a prolonged period. And not when you're not used to it. Her life here is with you, Junior. But we'll ensure she has company while you're away. It's going to make a world of difference."

I need to understand better, I say. When you say she'll have company, do you mean you're hiring her an assistant or something?

He chuckles, glances at Hen. "No, it's not an assistant. It's better than that. You'd be amazed at what's possible. It started with the virtual-reality peak thirty or so years ago, but VR has run its course. It's obsolete, as you know. This is next level, and it is fully guaranteed, in every way."

You're not putting her into a VR pod for months, I say, because that's not carrying on as normal, that's not living. That's a coma, that's—

"Absolutely not! We're taking her husband away, and what we're going to do is fair and natural."

Okay, I say. And what the hell does that mean?

"It means we're going to replace you."

I want to hit him. Punch him in the face. Break his nose. This is not at all what I'd expected. I've considered a lot of possibilities and various scenarios over the last few days, over the last two years, but not this. This wasn't a consideration.

No, I say. Fuck you.

"Junior," says Hen. "Take it easy."

"Junior," echoes Terrance, "I need you to calm down."

You fucking calm down! What the fuck are you talking about?

"Just hear me out. We're developing a replacement to fill the void you're going to leave behind. It's not somebody else. It's not a real person. It's a biomechanical duplicate. That duplicate will live here, with Henrietta. It will do what you do. It will be you, essentially."

No, I don't think this is a good idea, I say. I don't like this.

"This is a lot for him to take in," says Hen.

"Think about your wife, Junior. This is better than the alternative. You live in the middle of nowhere. Do you really want her to be all alone for all that time? What if someone came out here and wanted to harm her? Then what? This duplicate will be there for her. It will be just like you, identical in every conceivable way. It will be here to keep your place, hold your place, to help your wife get through this. And when you return—"

This is fucking crazy. It's insane. It can't be just like me, I say. That's stupid and impossible.

"It's not. It's more possible than you can imagine. The replacement will be just like you."

"Just like you," says Hen. "In every way. Hard to imagine."

I'm having trouble understanding this, I say. Is it real, this replacement? You said it's not a human replacement, so what is it?

"It's complex. I'm not an engineer, but to explain it very crassly: It's been designed with our most advanced computer software and produced using a 3D printer. We've been working with prototypes for a decade or so. It's remarkable. You can't tell the difference. Even Hen will not be able to look at it and see any disparity between the replacement and the original. There's nothing distinct. Not in any way."

This is a joke, I say. I don't want a robot look-alike coming to live with my wife.

"It's not a robot. It's a new kind of self-determining life-form, an advanced automated computer program. A conflation of life and science. If you prefer, think of it as a very sophisticated, dynamic hologram with living tissue, with volume and a body. In the old days, you would have left a photograph of yourself for Hen. This is the next step."

I turn to Hen.

What do you think? I ask.

FOE

"I think it sounds hard to believe and weird and startling. It must be even weirder for you to hear it."

"You need to trust me on this," says Terrance.

Do I have a choice? Can we decline this? What if we decide we don't want this replacement?

"Don't you see how great this will be? You won't have to worry about Hen now. You can focus on your trip knowing that she will be taken care of. And when you return, everything will continue on as though you'd never been away."

"That's right," says Hen, her voice clearly laced with frustration. "You don't have to worry about me now."

"Development has already started. And I'm going to need your help to finish it. Especially your help, Junior."

That's why you're staying here, isn't it? Does it have to do with this replacement?

"It does, yes. I'm here to gather and observe, to collect information. Everything I notice about you can help ensure the program is wholly realistic and lifelike. They've already codified all your screen correspondence, which is a good start. But while I'm here, Junior, I want you to think of the program as an understudy to you, as if you were both actors in a play. Everything you can tell me about yourself will be a help. No detail is inconsequential. For example, what did you have for breakfast yesterday morning?"

Fuck off, I say.

"Junior, please. Come on. Your breakfast. Yesterday. What did you have?"

Hen nods at me, indicating I should go along with it. For her sake, I do.

Coffee, toast, I say.

He types something on his screen.

103

"You see? Was that so hard? That's helpful. It seems trivial, but it isn't. How you're feeling, what you're thinking, every single detail will make a difference."

"I need some air," says Hen. She doesn't wait for a response from either of us. She just stands and brusquely walks out of the room, out the front door.

"Junior, we're going to need you to be strong here, okay? This isn't easy for her. The faster you can accept this, the less friction there'll be going forward. We're all in this together. Do this for her."

He's looking at me more intensely than he ever has before. Gone is that goofy intellectual shtick. All his visits have been leading to this point right now. Finally, something real. I get it.

It's true, I have been worrying about Hen, I think, about her being here all alone for so long. I just don't know if I want to accept this . . . thing . . . as a solution. How *can* I accept it? How can I accept being replaced?

"I need to grab a few things from my car," Terrance announces. "And then we'll get started."

What do you mean get started? Already?

"Junior," he says, standing, "you still don't you get it, do you? It's already started."

ACT TWO

OCCUPANCY

M emories. More of them. Memories I'd forgotten, or ones I thought I'd forgotten, ones I didn't even know I had stored away, have been returning.

I remember the very first night when Hen heard the noises. It was probably six months, maybe eight, after Terrance's first visit. She wasn't sleeping very well then. Many of those nights I'd wake up to find her lying on her back in bed, looking up at the ceiling, or at me. Some nights she wouldn't be in the bed at all. On this night she was the one who woke me up.

"Junior," she was saying, shaking my arm. "Junior. Wake up."

What? What is it? I asked.

"Can you hear it? Can you hear that?"

I'm asleep. What is it?

"Listen," she said.

I lay there, still half asleep, motionless, listening. The house was quiet. I told her so.

"I've been hearing it the last few nights, that noise. But tonight it's the worst. It sounds like a scratching in the walls."

You're probably dreaming, I said. Go back to sleep.

A minute later, maybe longer, she was waking me again.

"There, you hear that? I think it's the beetles. There's more of them. You must have heard that," she said.

But I hadn't. I'd been asleep. Like Hen should have been, too.

T errance returns from gathering some of his things from the car, carrying them directly upstairs. He insists that the three of us sit in the living room again. He has some "general questions," mostly for me, but he says he'd like Hen there as well. In case she has anything to add.

"Is it ever eerie at home?" Terrance asks.

Eerie? No, I say. It's home. This is my home.

"Maybe the odd time," Hen says. "But there are some good things about the quiet."

We're here for a reason, I say. There's a lot to like about this life.

"It's what we're used to," says Hen. "That's definitely true."

"It's just, I don't know. I haven't been here long enough to say. I just think it might get to me. A little bit. Mentally, I mean. Probably because I'm not used to it."

That's what everyone from the city thinks, I say. That's why everyone has left.

I give Hen a look, because she understands. She knows what it's like to be here, just the two of us, not bothered by all of that, all of that modern city life out there.

"I guess I feel what you're talking about sometimes," Hen says. "Just like . . . wondering what else is out there."

I'm surprised to hear her say this again. She told me this once before, but I thought it would go away and never resurface. It's hard to hear it didn't just fade. I don't get it. Hen loves the rural life.

"The thought of ever going somewhere new is scary," she says. "But isn't it good to scare yourself from time to time? It's so easy to get stuck in your own narrow rut. We convince ourselves they're paths to something else, contentment, but really they're just ruts going on forever."

We like it here just fine, I say.

Terrance changes the subject. "You play the piano," he says to Hen. "Correct?"

Hen plays it. She loves to play, and I love listening to her.

"Piano is a beautiful sound," he says.

"The tune is off," Hen says. "It's defective."

"Pardon me?" Terrance says.

"The piano. It's been here longer than us, so it's not in the best shape," she says. "It's not in tune."

But it helps her, I say. It's relaxing.

I think of her playing, and reach out to take her hand.

Music is therapeutic, I tell Terrance. I'm glad she has something that's hers. Something she can do that I can't.

"How have you guys been able to keep your chickens under the

110

livestock ban? And don't worry, I'm not going to tell anyone about a few chickens. As far as I'm concerned, that's not a big deal."

Nobody knows. There aren't many, I say. They were here when we got the place. I didn't want to get rid of them.

"I told him if he wanted to look after them, fine, but I have no interest in looking after them," says Hen. "I'm not interested in shoveling chicken shit. I told him he can pay the fine if we get caught."

"Well, that's fascinating," says Terrance. "You see? That's why we have these rambling conversations. It's illuminating, to talk about these things."

He starts typing something into his screen again. Notes, I guess.

"The more I learn, the more at home I feel," he says.

When there's finally a break in our conversation, Terrance stands.

"I think I better head up," he says, stretching his arms above his head. "Start to unpack, get some gear out. Set up a bit. Don't mind me."

Gear? What for? Do you have a lot of gear?

"No, not too much. Nothing you have to worry about. Just a few essentials to help with data collection and stuff."

"I'll show you your room," says Hen.

"Oh, Junior, here. Don't forget to take two of these."

He holds up a translucent pill bottle, shakes it.

"Here," he says. "Doctor's orders."

What are these? Painkillers?

"They should help," he says. "Yes."

My shoulder does hurt, but in a vague way. I hold my hand out and he tips two blue capsules into my palm.

"Those should do the trick."

They each take a couple of bags that Terrance had already carried in from the car and head upstairs. I get up very slowly, still feeling stiff and tender. I know I'm supposed to move around a bit. After all, it's not my legs that are injured. I clear the table. Without putting too much pressure on my bad shoulder, I attempt to wash the dirty dishes stacked beside the sink. The caked-on egg yolk is the hardest to get off. As long as I don't extend my arm, as long as I keep it anchored against my side, the pain isn't bad.

There's a strange man upstairs with my wife while I'm down here, washing dishes with one arm. But what can I do? How should I react? Just go along with everything, try to be passive and agreeable? Or should I be putting up more resistance against this whole process? Demanding more answers?

I hear Hen walking around upstairs, above me. I know it's her by her steps. The pace. The weight. It's amazing the ways we know someone after living with them as long as Hen and I have lived together. The time we've spent together: it's significant. I'll miss hearing those gentle steps when I'm gone. Hearing her steps is like hearing her talk; it's as recognizable as her voice.

Walking is nonverbal communication. Like I can tell if Hen's mad by her footsteps. Walking isn't as overt as other signals, like the way someone smells, their voice, their laugh, their facial expressions. Steps can be frivolous, but they're often distinct from person to person. Familiarity grows over time, slowly, inadvertently. I never tried to get to know her walk deliberately. This stuff happens unwittingly.

Terrance isn't married. I don't know if he understands marriage or how committed relationships function. You can't really understand a relationship until you live it, unless you're in it. That's part of what made everything so exciting for Hen and me. We were starting out together, we'd committed to each other, but we still didn't know all those small details about each other at first.

Living with someone can't be simulated or rehearsed. It has to be experienced, in real time. There is no substitute for shared involvement, for creating actual memories. Like, I know how Hen blows her nose. I've never thought about it until now, but I do. I know the cadence, the rhythm. She does it in the same tempo every time.

These observations—her footsteps, how she blows her nose—they're like little secrets.

I'll miss her steps, and the way she blows her nose. I wonder what else I'll miss. I wonder what she privately knows about me that I might not even know about myself. What will she miss about me when I'm gone?

I hear a door open, more walking above me. Hen's laugh. I can tell it's sincere. She has a fake laugh, and a real one, like everyone. That's something else I've grown to recognize. This laugh is real.

I've known him for a few years now, been aware of him, but when I stop to think about it, I still don't know much about Terrance. I'm not only referring to his personality and nature, but all the ways he exists, both consciously and involuntarily. This is the stuff that requires time. Time together. I don't know how he walks through a house at night or what he thinks about as he tries to fall asleep.

I know where he works. I'm familiar with his face. I recognize his voice. I know his smile. That's about it. That's not a lot. Those details are all aspects he can control to shape my perception. But now he's here, living with us, in our house, eating our food, using our bathroom, sleeping in our guest bed. Watching me, us.

What does he really want? Just to observe? To talk to me? Or something else?

She laughs again, harder this time. He must have said something funny. He doesn't strike me as a funny guy. I can't hear what they're saying. I set the last dish from the sink into the drying rack and run my hands through the soapy water, ensuring there's no cutlery left in the bottom. I lift the plug, letting the water drain out.

I can't believe everything that's happened since these plates were dirtied. It makes me feel like a different person. It's not just today, the last few weeks. It's incorporating the addition of new experiences and information, fitting it in to what my life was before Terrance showed up that night more than two years ago, when I first saw those green headlights at the end of the lane.

Our house is the same old house. I look at my dripping, soapy hands. The same hands I've always had. All is the same, all is unchanged, but as of today, right now, everything feels completely different.

Hen appears at the kitchen door, then comes up beside me. "He's getting settled," she says.

I've been thinking, I say. It's not an optimal situation, but we really have to try. We have to make the best of this. We'll get through it. He shouldn't be here too long. Then it'll just be us again. For a while. Before I go, I mean. Did he say yet how long he'd be here?

"Until Friday."

Okay. At least it's just him, and not a bunch of them. One stranger, no matter how nice he pretends to be, is plenty for me.

I sling the tea towel over my sore shoulder.

Do you think he's nice?

"He is what he is."

Do you consider him a stranger?

"I wouldn't say that, not at this point."

Really? I say. Think about it. He is.

I lean closer, lower my voice.

We don't know him. Not really. It's just that whenever we see him, something significant has happened. There's big news and revelations. So it feels like we know him better than we do.

"I don't feel like I know him *well*," she says. "That's not what I'm saying. I just don't think he's a complete stranger. I know him better than I know a lot of people. But never mind. You're entitled to your opinion."

I put a hand on her shoulder.

You feeling okay?

"Yeah," she says. "I'm tired."

Feels like he's been here forever, doesn't it? I say. Months, even. Honestly, I feel like my internal clock has been all messed up. Maybe it's the accident. What were you guys talking about up there?

"When?"

When I was doing the dishes just now.

"You shouldn't be doing the dishes. Your shoulder."

What were you guys talking about?

"I can't remember. I was showing him his room, then I was in our room. Nothing specific. Why?"

Is Terrance funny?

"Like, is he a funny guy?"

Yeah.

"I don't know. Do you get that feeling? That he's funny?"

No, just wondering. You've talked to him more than I have, that's all.

"I'm sure he'd tell you a joke if that's what you're wanting."

I'm sure he would, I say. If that's what I wanted.

She pauses, looks at me, then turns to leave.

Wait, I say.

She stops.

Does it seem weird to you that I was found out in that field? That the doctor got here so fast?

"Not really," she says, turning toward me. "Clearly OuterMore has a vested interest in keeping you healthy."

They were there before I was, before whatever happened to me. I wonder if . . . I wonder if maybe they were following me, I say.

"I thought you said you don't remember anything."

I don't. But I . . . I don't know. Maybe I remember a little. Someone stopped me from getting to that barn fire. Someone knocked me down.

"You hit your head when you fell. I'm not surprised you're confused." She reaches a hand out to me, touches my wrist. It feels good, her touch—calming.

Thanks, I say. You know how to make me feel better. Recently it's been hard for me, hard not to feel weird and unsure about things.

"Junior?"

What?

"I'm going to say something, okay?" I feel her hand squeeze my wrist harder. "I know you so well. I really do. Things have changed over the course of our relationship. We've both changed. You probably feel the same about me. Change in relationships is normal. But, even as things changed for us, after we got married and moved here, I still feel like I *know you* so well. I know you better than ever. I think that's part of the problem. When you start a relationship, you just have to go all in, and it's based on a mix of hope and belief that you do know who you're marrying and what it's going to be like. But you can't really know how it will work out. Not until you live it. At some point the hope turns into constancy and comprehension and then repetition. It's so . . . severe. The predictability of everything we've done. It's become the new truth for us. Which for me isn't comforting. It's the opposite."

I'm about to reply when she releases her hand and raises it to stop me. She doesn't want to hear what I have to say.

"I want to talk now. And I want you to listen. You have these traits, a way of being that's fundamental to you, and it can be exhausting. I wonder if that's just an inherent part of who you are or if it's part of us in this relationship. And maybe I shouldn't be sensitive about this, or even wonder if it's unique to our relationship. I know you think you're being nice when you say that you don't know what you'd be without me, but I feel like I'm not here only to help you feel secure in your life, or to offer you support so you can then do whatever it is you want to do. I don't know if you understand any of this, but I've been thinking about this for a long time. Sometimes I feel drained. Sometimes I feel trapped."

She's serious about this. It's in her eyes, her voice, everything. She sounds tired again. I should listen to what she's saying. I know things haven't always been perfect between us, but I don't like that I've caused this distress. It's not good. I feel bad.

I'm sorry if I've—

"Stop," she says. "Don't apologize, please. That's not what I want from you. You're listening to me, and that's a help. I've never felt like I could bring this up. Even that, the fact I don't want to bring this up, is upsetting to me. But I'm glad I have now."

Hey, why don't you play the piano tonight. Maybe that will help.

I don't know where it comes from, this idea. But I know it's good when she plays.

She blinks, sighs. "I hadn't really thought about it."

I think it seems appropriate. I think you'll feel better.

She turns and leaves.

I stay where I am. She doesn't say anything else. It takes a few minutes for Hen to get down to the cellar, take the cover off, and start playing her song.

I 've never had to sleep in this disagreeable position—reclined, half lying, half sitting. I already miss lying down, stretching in a big, soft bed beside my wife. There are times when I like to reach out, with a hand or foot, and touch her. My skin brushing against hers. After being forced to sleep in a chair, I'll never take her presence for granted again. I miss having her body beside me.

Hen played the piano for a while, but not for very long. She stopped abruptly, midsong. I'm glad she played. I know how much it helps her. I like hearing it, too. It's reassuring. Even on that faulty piano, she plays gently, beautifully. I was close to falling asleep as she played but didn't quite get there. Now that she's stopped and gone up to bed, I'm awake again, involuntarily alert, sitting here in the heat of the house, my mind racing.

There are certain moods, like tonight's, that remind me how much is beyond my own intentions and desires, how much I can't control, even within myself. I forget that sometimes. I can fall into the habit of believing I can regulate everything. My hope right now is to sleep, to rest, to recover. But my goal doesn't matter. What I want is irrelevant.

Terrance's room is right above me. I can hear him getting settled. It sounds like he's still unpacking. I would have thought he'd have gone to bed already. What's so important, so urgent that he has to stay up this late? He's walking around, back and forth, maybe between the bed and where I imagine his bags are, and the closet.

He's right about my memory, my thoughts. He said it would be understandable if my mind was racing these days. Since he's been back and given us the news of my forthcoming departure, my mind is more alive, more alert, more awake than it has been in a long time. Maybe more awake than ever, as if the news has acted as a stimulant. Minute to minute I can sense the change within me. It's an exciting feeling, as if I've been neglecting an entire section of my brain that I've only just discovered.

He said this might happen. He said there might be some extreme feelings, ups and downs. That I might feel energetic and productive one moment, and sullen and forlorn the next. We still don't know much about the Installation and what life will be like. That's what happens with news like this, shocking news and the expectation of change ahead. He warned me not to overdo anything, not to let my thoughts get the better of me, to restrain myself.

Sitting here, alone in the dark, I can't help but think about the early days with Hen, when everything was new between us. I'm trying not to obsess, but it's hard not to. I know this to be true: Back then I didn't worry. It was simple. We didn't fight, no drawn-out arguments or long periods of silence. We were new, and I was enamored.

The news of my departure has been harder on Hen. I can see it in her demeanor. She is susceptible to doubt, more so than I am. I was anxious before, but now . . . now I'm feeling a growing energy, a realization of purpose. Meanwhile, she seems scattered, either too attentive to me or completely emotionally absent.

Terrance is right. I should use these days before I go. I'm going to be productive and efficient. I'm going to focus on what needs to be done.

He's walking again, slowly, pacing. I can hear the creaking floor and another strange noise. It's coming from up there, too, from his room. I'm not at all tired yet, and I won't be able to fall asleep. I'm wired. I'm going to investigate further, to find out what the noise is.

I head upstairs. I knock on Terrance's closed door. It opens partway. He leans out, shirtless. Like me, he's wearing only boxer shorts. He's holding something in one hand. He's lean, more muscular than I thought. He's breathing heavier than usual, as if he was just exercising. His long hair isn't in the usual ponytail, but falls down either side of his face.

"Junior. Everything okay?" he asks.

He looks distracted. I can see past him just enough to get a glimpse of his equipment. There's lots of it. More than I thought. More than I recall him carrying in.

That's a lot of stuff, I say.

I'm seeing his full collection of bags for the first time. A few boxes. There's a tripod in mid assembly.

"Yup, got everything in now. Shouldn't take me too long to get this stuff up and running. It's all top-of-the-line."

What's going on? Why do you need all this equipment?

"To gather information. I told you that. I just have to set it up."

What's involved in setting up?

"Nothing too extensive. Putting some of this together. Hen told me there's a good spot in the attic for Dotty. She said it's quiet up there, which is good."

Dotty?

"Sorry, one of our computers. I'll use it to record the more formal interviews we'll do. It's a bit bigger, so I'm going to set it up and just leave it there. We'll go to it when we need to. The rest of the equipment is smaller, lighter. You won't even notice it."

I wonder if Hen has seen all of his gear. I point at a small device in his hand. It's about the size of a coffee mug.

What's that?

"Yeah, that's what I'm talking about. That's just your basic recorder. I'll probably put this in the kitchen."

You're going to record the kitchen?

"I'll make sure it's not in your way."

It'll be running? All the time?

"Yeah, once I get it set up."

Why the kitchen? I don't get it. This is crazy.

"It's data collection, Junior. The kitchen is an important place in any house."

It's also a private place, I think, the place where Hen and I have coffee in the mornings, eat dinner in the evenings. Where we talk, or used to. It's not a lab.

"We want this to be as thorough as possible. We need it to be. For Hen's sake more than anything. This is all about learning and understanding. Actually, since you're here, can you give me a quick hand with this?"

He turns back into his room, opens the door fully, and bends over one of the boxes, removing a long, skinny, black metal rod. I walk into the room.

"Here," he says. "Hold on to this."

I take it. It's lighter than it looks.

"Just a second, I have to find an attachment. It should have been packed in the same bag, but it wasn't. It's around here somewhere."

What is this?

"That's Flotsam."

Flotsam?

"Most of the cameras have names. Engineer humor. You get used to it. Flotsam is attached to the retractable boom. Jetsam's around here somewhere, too."

It looks excessive, I say. And invasive.

"I'm not a tech expert, but it's all pretty standard and user-friendly. You need a computer-science degree to design it, not to use it. Here it is," he says.

He takes a small clasp from another bag.

"If you're good holding that for one more minute, I'll just get the lens on."

As he's fiddling with the lens on the end of the boom, I look down into the bag. Lots of pieces of equipment, some spare-looking parts, extras, clamps. And then something catches my eye underneath the metal. A photo. Not on a screen, but an old, paper photo, a printed image.

"Great," he says, stepping beside me, suddenly zipping the bag shut. "Here, I'll take that now."

He grabs the rod from my hand.

I can't be sure. And maybe I'm just tired, but I think that was me. The photo. But from a few years ago. Many years ago, in fact. I can barely recognize myself, and yet I know that was me. Me, standing there, arms at my side, wearing a blue-and-white plaid shirt. I have no recollection of that shirt. I have no memory of such a photo ever being taken. Has so much changed since then?

Terrance has assembled a boom that he puts down by the bed.

"Actually, no worries, I can finish this up on my own tomorrow," he says, ushering me back out into the hall. "Thanks for the help."

Sure, I say. I thought I heard something up here, from your room. That's why I came up in the first place.

"Sorry about that, buddy. I'm just excited to get all this ready. Did it wake you?"

I wasn't asleep yet.

"I'll keep it down. I think we both, Hen and I, probably just assumed you would't notice, being downstairs and all. And I like to work at night. It helps me sleep."

Are you stressed about this?

"No, no. Definitely not. Not at all. Are you kidding? No, I'm excited. I couldn't be happier. You're doing so well."

I try to peer past him into the room again, but can't see anything with him in the way. He's obstructing my entry.

"It's a new place for me. New bed. And you weren't kidding about the heat. That's all. I'm realizing I don't need as much sleep as most people do. I'm starting to think it's overrated, for me anyway."

Everyone needs to sleep, I say.

"Is that what you think? Interesting." He takes a step out into the hall and closes the door behind him.

"Sleeping is interesting," he says. "It's not efficient. There's always room to make people more efficient. Eating, communicating, sleeping—what if we didn't need to do any of it?"

But why? Why wouldn't we want to do those things? Why would not doing them make us better?

He pauses, thinks. When he speaks, he speaks slowly, carefully.

"It's about efficiency. It would expedite the process of evolution.

If it will all end up happening eventually. Why not help it along, if we can?"

Are you *helping* it along? I ask.

It seems more like interfering, I think.

"I'm glad you asked that, because what we have to do is change our way of thinking about evolution." He puts a hand on his chest. "The only constant quality of humanness is that we adapt. Always. So imagine that in a thousand years we won't need to sleep more than twenty minutes a night: that would signify a progression. If we can get there sooner, I think we have an obligation to try. We need to push the boundaries. Think about what we could do with an extra six or seven hours each day. It's astounding."

I don't know if I find it astounding or concerning.

This is your area. It's what you do, I say. I just don't feel all that excited about the kind of forced progress you're talking about. Sleeping is just one of those things we have to do, and I'm okay with that. I'm used to it. It's what I know.

Terrance laughs as I say this. He laughs hard, harder than I've heard him laugh before.

"There's still no definitive answer to the question of why we have to sleep. But I can assure you that we're studying it. Carefully."

We sleep to rest. To give our bodies a chance to recover. Dreaming, too.

"Dreaming, yes. Do you dream a lot?"

Doesn't everyone? I answer.

"Sleeping is about a lot things. It could be about decluttering our brains. In order to acquire new information and process it, like you've had to do the last couple of days. We have to grow synapses between neurons in our brain. Brains need rest to do this."

He's speaking almost in a whisper, as if our impromptu discussion might wake Hen. She's asleep down the hall, but her door is ajar.

"There's no way we could function if we didn't forget the vast majority of new information we acquire throughout the day. In other words, Junior, we sleep so we can forget."

I consider what he's just said.

I don't want to forget, I say.

"Yes," he says, raising his voice, "then you're with me. You see? That's why we're studying sleep and memory. You have such an important role in all of this. You don't fully realize how, but you're very important to us."

He's been trying to make me feel special and unique since he first arrived, but it's not working.

I just want what's best for me and my wife, I say. I want to live right, to be a good person, to make a difference, even if it's only a small one.

"You want to make your mark."

Sure, I guess I do, I say.

"You don't have to worry about that anymore. Trust me when I say that you are making a mark. You're making a huge contribution. You have no idea how vital you are, how valuable. For now, just know that it's good for you to sleep as much as possible, to be rested. Especially since your accident." He pauses. "This is a bit of a tangent, but do you ever think about consciousness?"

Consciousness? Not really.

"But you are aware of it, right? What it is. The world that's alive inside your own head, which is distinct from my own, distinct from Hen's. Not to get too nerdy, but pretty much since the time of Descartes we've been aware of the two distinct realms—mind and matter."

Yeah, I say. Sure. I haven't thought about it much. But it's interesting.

"Good, good. I'm glad you think so, too. I know it's late. But since we're talking, can I ask you something?"

He's whispering again. I'm finding it hard to hear, and we're standing close together.

What do you want to ask?

"If Hen"—he motions toward our bedroom with his eyes—"was the same as she is now, in every way, but was a bit less physically attractive in one significant way, do you think you would have married her?"

I'm caught off guard by the question, but I don't want to show that I am, so I don't hesitate with my answer.

Of course, I say. I love Hen. Hen's my wife. She'll be with me forever. I've always loved her. I'll always love her.

"I know that. I know. I don't doubt you love her very much. That's not *really* what I'm asking, though. Are you sure you would have married her? Committed to her forever? Think about it. Does her appearance not mean anything to you? Is that what you're saying? That what she looks like is irrelevant?"

It's such a blunt and tactless question. It seems out of line with everything else we've talked about. I feel a trickle of sweat slide down my spine.

I'm saying, to me, no matter what, she would still be Hen.

"Would she, though? Would she be the Hen you fell in love with? What about this: What if she looked exactly as she does right now, but she was a bit less intelligent? Would she still be Hen?"

That's just stupid. It's a stupid question. Hen is Hen.

I feel a pinch in my shoulder and bring my hand up to it. He's watching me, making me aware once again that he's here to monitor me and learn.

"I'm sorry. I shouldn't be keeping you up. It's unfair of me. I'll keep the noise down. No more noise tonight, I promise."

I figure right now is the time to ask him something, something that's been nagging me ever since Hen brought it up.

Have you heard any strange sounds? Like a light scratching in the walls?

"I haven't," he says. "Is everything okay?"

Fine, just wondering. Good night.

"Sleep well, Junior. Big day tomorrow, big day. And keep in mind: soon our observation period will be over, and then you won't have anything to worry about again. I promise. Everything will be taken care of. Just hang in there a bit longer. Only a couple more days."

He turns back into his room and closes the door with a soft, almost imperceptible click.

"Good morning, Junior."

I open my eyes. Blink several times.

"How did you sleep?"

Terrance is standing over me. Grinning, rested, and fresh. He's holding a cup of coffee. I can smell it. He has my favorite mug.

Morning, I say, squinting up at him. What time is it?

"Just before eight. Thought it best to let you sleep a bit longer today. How's the shoulder?"

Fine, I say. Where's Hen?

"Gone to work. She left about ten minutes ago. It's just you and me, buddy."

I sit up, wincing from the pain in my shoulder. Terrance hands me the mug. It's hot, strong, the way I like it. I didn't think I would ever fall asleep on this chair last night. When I came back downstairs, I was wide-awake. I walked around in the dark. I went onto the porch for a bit. I paced around the living room. I couldn't get comfortable. I was restless. I considered going upstairs to see if Hen was awake, too. I couldn't hear anything up there, so decided against it.

Eventually, I sat back down in the chair, closed my eyes. I listened to the house. I don't know if I slept at all, but I guess I must have, at least for a bit.

"You were right out. We thought we might wake you when we ate breakfast, but you slept right through it. No nightmares?"

No, I say. Why would I have nightmares?

He doesn't answer.

"Good?" he says. "Did I get that right?"

What?

"The coffee? Strong, with cream and sugar. That's how you take it, right?"

How did you know?

"Hen filled me in."

It's good, I say.

"This, too, don't forget," he says, handing me a pill.

I accept it reluctantly, swallowing it with another sip. I swing my legs around and off the chair. I stand up with a yawn. I walk over to the window and look out. Another hot, sunny day. The usual thick morning haze. Maybe we'll get a storm. Hopefully. Cut the humidity.

I grab my screen, turn on the weather forecast.

The temperature will remain steady, but the relative humidity continues to climb. . . .

Terrance is watching me, watching me as I listen to the weather forecast. He interrupts.

"Sweating is less useful when it's so humid," Terrance says. "Too bad we don't have a better way of cooling off."

I can already feel the sweat starting around my temples. It'll just get worse as the day goes on. The more he talks about it, the more I'm aware of it.

I should probably get some grain to the chickens, I say, buttoning my shirt.

"Already done."

I stop.

"I figured since I was up I could be of some assistance."

You already fed the chickens? That's my job.

"That's okay. No worries. I did it for you. They went pretty wild for the feed. I know it's still early, but we have limited time, and I was hoping that if I did your chores, we could get started right away."

You mean with an interview?

"Now that Hen's gone, we won't be interrupted."

I wish he'd mentioned this last night. That we'd be starting first thing. I was looking forward to getting out to the barn, getting away.

Fine, I say.

"Are you hungry yet, or are you okay with the coffee? Hen said you usually start with your coffee and breakfast later."

Coffee's good, I say. I might just hit the toilet first.

"Right. Of course, of course. I'll just wait here. Take your time."

I 've escaped. I've found a way to get away from him, at least for a moment. To get away from the questions, the staring, the attention. It's a relief to be on my own, even if I'm jammed in our small washroom.

I'm looking at my reflection in the mirror. There I am. Same as always but somehow sagging, tired, older-looking. I notice a long strand of blond hair in the sink. It's a single hair. It shouldn't bother me. I've already brushed my teeth, splashed some cold water onto my face. I look like I haven't slept at all, not a minute. The energy I was feeling yesterday has dissipated overnight.

I pick up the hair and hold it in the light close to my face. I turn it over. I drop it into the toilet. I get down on my knees. I bring my face down as close to the floor tiles as I can. I want to see if there are more hairs. My nose is hovering an inch or so above the floor. Nothing. I shift, peer behind the toilet, running my hand around the base as if

I'm searching for a lost ring. It's cool to the touch and wet back there. Condensation beads on the side. The toilet itself is sweating like the rest of us.

Other than the hair, there's no sign of him in here. Terrance hasn't left his toothbrush in our holder. That's good. The towel Hen gave him isn't hanging with the others. He must have brought it back to his room. His room is right next door to the bathroom. Right through that wall behind the toilet. He's probably wondering what's taking me so long up here. I twist the tap back on to let the water run.

I stand in front of the toilet and pee. I look into the bowl before flushing. It's a dark yellow. I must be dehydrated. I should drink more.

I wash my hands. I open the medicine cabinet and take out the roll of floss. Hen is the regular flosser. Or so she claims. I don't use it often. I close the cabinet and pull out a long line. I wrap one end around my left index finger and look into the mirror.

I wrap the other end of the floss around my right index finger and bring it up to my mouth. I open wide. I slip the floss between two teeth near the back. I bring it down in between the gums, forcefully. I move it back and forth, applying increased pressure. I keep doing it until it feels uncomfortable, until I taste the metallic flavor of blood. I don't stop. I keep going. I increase the force. The discomfort becomes pain. My eyes tear up. My mouth fills with blood. I spit into the sink and watch the mixture of blood and saliva trickle toward the drain.

I know I should feel shame or disgust, but that's not what I feel when I see my own blood against the white porcelain. I feel good. I feel awake. Alert and alive.

I emerge from the bathroom as though everything is normal. Terrance ushers me upstairs to the attic, walking behind me without speaking. That's where he will conduct the interview. The interview I don't feel at all like doing. I don't want him here, in my house, invading my space. I don't want to answer his questions, but I feel I have to. It's presented as a choice, but is it? Do I really have a choice?

"Okay, Junior. Whenever you're ready. Visuals are set. Can you say something? I'm setting the sound levels."

The attic is the hottest place in the house. I don't get why Terrance thought it would be the best place to do these interviews. There's empty space and it's quiet, but it's not like there are a lot of distractions downstairs.

He's already set up two folding chairs for us. What's most unusual is the placement of the chairs. Instead of sitting facing each other, I'm facing the wall, and Terrance is positioned behind me. He tells me to sit and relax. I sit. And I hear him take a seat behind me. I can't see him, only hear him. A single lens on a tripod is beside him, facing me.

What should I say? Can you hear me? Hello. Hello.

"Perfect, got it. Don't worry, Junior. It's recording just fine. All good. Okay, so tell us about something."

I want you gone. I'm not your friend. I want you to leave, I think. Get out of my house.

Like what? I ask.

"Whatever you want. Really, anything."

I don't know. What do you expect to hear?

"How about work? Where do you work; what do you do, Junior?"

He already knows what I do, but I guess I'm supposed to offer more details.

When I'm not injured like I am now, I work at the feed mill. Most of the work is done at the south end of the loading dock. That's my post.

I pause. I don't know what else to say. I don't want to say a lot more.

"Elaborate. I'm listening, but I'm not going to talk. Just tell me more. Whatever comes to mind."

The grain comes every day, at all times of day. I could have taken a different position, asked for a job with less lifting, less physical work. But I'm used to the work. I like working hard. I don't like sitting around all day or wasting time like some guys. Mornings are busiest at the mill. They go by the fastest. I've always said it's better to be busy than to be idle.

"This is great, Junior. Tell me more."

Should I tell you about the grain? I ask.

"Yes, sure. Tell me about the grain."

It comes in bagged or free. The bagged grain is easiest to deal with. It's unloaded from trucks on wooden skids. I move the skids one at a time using a forklift. I move them from the loading bay to the pit. Everything goes to the pit first. It gets divided and moved around from there.

The free grain gets dumped directly into portable hoppers. Then it has to be bagged. We do that in the bagging stalls. It's easy, mindless work. The boredom can get to you if you let it. It gets pretty dusty, too. You don't even know it, but it's there—like a layer or fine coating. You can go crazy bagging grain.

"Do you remember a time when there were actual farms around here, with animals?"

I think about it.

No, I don't, I say.

"I guess those mega farms can be pretty nasty places."

The poultry farms are the worst.

"You've been to one?"

No, I haven't, I say. But that's what I've heard. They say they're awful places.

"Do they?"

They pack so many birds into each building. It's wrong. They have elevators in those places, dozens of floors of birds living on top of one another. There's zero fresh air. No natural light. They're supposed to be vented, but they aren't.

"You know a lot about this."

I guess so, yeah. You can learn a lot by listening. The vents are always breaking and don't get repaired right away. No one gives a shit about the vents or light or the birds.

"So you talk about this stuff at work? Is that how you know about it?"

I don't talk much at work. Not usually. But I listen.

"And the guys you've worked with, they've told you stories."

Yeah. I overhear stuff.

"So, these are firsthand accounts. And from those accounts, you're forming your own opinions? Your own judgments? Or would you say these are the judgments of the guys at work?"

One of the guys who used to work at a poultry farm said chickens' brains are smaller than his thumb. *The privilege of being human is that our brains are big enough to decide the fate of other creatures.* That's what he said. Then he laughed.

"Did he tell you anything else?"

Bacteria and fungi outbreaks aren't uncommon in those places. Lethargy and disorientation are the norm for the birds. Workers are supposed to wear masks, goggles, and gloves the whole time they're inside the poultry barns. There are all sorts of ugly microscopic parasites that harm any kind of poultry. Very few birds, if any, are healthy.

"Why do you think you're telling me about this?"

I don't know, I say, after considering his question.

"That's interesting, Junior. It really is. Have you ever shared this with Hen? Or is it just that this information, this memory is only coming back to you now?"

I don't know, I say.

I hear him making some noises on his screen behind me. But he doesn't say anything.

"You must be happy to work at the mill. Sounds like the right spot for you."

Was I happy? Am I? Maybe, I think. How does anyone feel about their work? We work because we have to.

It's just grain, feed, grain, feed, I say. All day. Time keeps moving. I've always thought that was a good thing. Until recently. I'm not so sure now. Is it good? For time to go by fast? And just the other day, that made me think about time in a different way. Why do we live in the time we do? What if—

"That's enough for now, Junior. Thanks. You've done very well. One last question and then you can have a break. Can you close your eyes for a second?"

I close them.

"Okay. Now, can you see?"

You just asked me to close my eyes.

"I know, but I don't mean it quite like that. Think about what I'm asking. Can you still see with your eyes closed?"

I can't see you or what's happening in the room right now.

"I know that. Can you still see anything?"

I wait. I keep my eyes closed. I clear my mind. I focus. What am I supposed to see?

Yes, I say. I can.

"What can you see?"

Right now?

"Yes, right now."

Hen.

Terrance indicates that our chat is finished. I get up and walk downstairs. I feel spent, distressed, perplexed by the interview. The atmosphere was unexpectedly tense. I wasn't prepared to talk so much. But once in the chair, I couldn't stop myself. His questions, his silence. It's as if they were designed to make the information flow from me. The more I'm around him, the less I trust him.

Outside, I follow our narrow dirt path to the barn. I unhook the chain, lift the wooden latch, and enter the barn. The chickens are roving around aimlessly, as they do. Some peer up at me, others ignore me completely. I don't need to, but I top up their grain anyway. I find my thoughts continue to spiral, and instead of feeling better, I'm feeling worse. My shoulder aches. Why did I tell him about those poultry farms? I look down at my own chickens. They aren't tortured like on those farms. These chickens are fed properly. They're taken care of. They have space. Freedom.

From the single, small window in the barn, I look back at the house. I see movement upstairs in Terrance's room. He's in there. I continue watching until his blinds close. I'm glad I have the barn. I'm glad I have this space I can come to when I don't want to be in the house, when I need a break and some solitude, some time to think. I'm glad I have the chickens to look after, that I take care of them as thoughtfully as I do. I know them very well. They're familiar, predictable.

I stroll around the back of the barn, wander into the canola fields. Terrance's interviews have set something in motion within me that hasn't quite come to a full stop. Doesn't life have to be determined by each individual, and be involved to be legitimate? Doesn't there have to be an element of challenge and progression?

It makes me think about the Installation. Is that my calling? My challenge? Is that the progression that I'm being offered? What if someone else had been selected to go in my place? My life would have taken a different course, naturally. What if my inclusion wasn't a lottery at all, that it was preordained? I should ask Terrance about this, put him on the hot seat for once.

When I return to the house, Terrance is still upstairs. I call up to him.

Hello!

No answer.

I walk over to my chair in the living room. I pick up my screen. Without thinking about it, I call Hen at work. She answers on the third ring.

Hey, I say. It's me. I . . .

"What is it? You don't usually call me at work. What's up?"

I can hear concern in her voice.

We talked for a while this morning, I say. I mean, I did. Terrance got me talking. A lot. Now he's up in his room. Hen. It's weird. It's all weird. I don't know what's going on. With me. With him. With this.

"Weird how? What did you talk about?"

Mostly about work. But, it was . . . strange. I just tried to give him what he asked for. I tried to act relaxed. To say what came to mind. I don't understand what the point is.

She's quiet. She's not saying anything, but I can hear background noise, probably her coworkers.

How's work? I ask.

"Busy," she says. "Same old."

I've been thinking. Maybe we should tell someone about what's happening. Tell them about Terrance, why he's here, and about Outer-More and where I'm going.

"I'm not sure that's such a good idea," Hen answers.

Why not? Doesn't it seem creepy to you that—

I hear a creak and turn around. Terrance is standing behind me, only a few feet away. I had no idea he'd come downstairs. He made no sound until right now.

"Junior? What is it?" she says.

Nothing. I should probably get going.

"Okay, see you later."

I end the call and set my screen back down on the table.

"How are the chickens, Junior?"

He knows where I have been. He probably watched me the whole time, watched me leave the house, watched me walk down the steps, out to the barn, and into it. That's what he's here to do.

The chickens are the same, I say. I gave them some more grain.

"Was that Hen you were speaking with?"

Yeah.

"Do you often call her at work?"

It depends, but no, not often.

"Everything okay?"

Yeah. She's busy.

"We have to make sure she's okay. That's the most important thing. I don't mind saying it to you, but let's keep this between us. Often what happens in these situations is that the partner who stays behind takes the brunt and has the hardest time coping."

Well, that's understandable, I say. It's not like this is an everyday occurrence.

"True. This situation is stressful, uncertain, new. We did a lot of research into how partners are affected by potential absence. And I've come in here and messed up your quiet routine, and I just want us to see eye to eye, to both make sure we keep Hen's welfare front of the mind. So if you think she's acting odd, or if she says anything to you that you find . . . disconcerting, it's best you tell me. Right away. Has she said anything unusual to you?"

No, I say.

"Good. Junior, I'm sorry. Before we talked this morning, there was something I forgot. It's my fault. It's not a big deal, but it's best to do it now. It won't take a minute."

What is it?

"It's nothing. I just need to put something on you. A tiny sensor."

He holds up a light-brown pad between two fingers. It's thin, small, not much bigger than a coin and resembles a circular Band-Aid, pliable and soft.

"It's light and innocuous. You won't even feel it."

I don't want to wear that, I say.

"It's nothing. But it's important. It keeps track of your blood pressure, heart rate. Boring stuff like that."

How long am I supposed to keep it on?

He moves behind me. "You'll forget it's even there after thirty seconds, I promise."

I repeat my refusal but feel him press the sensor firmly into the middle of my neck, directly below my hairline. I feel a mild heat, a dull pinching sensation. I bring a hand up to the spot, touching it.

"That's it. That's all. It's done."

Will it stay on? Or is it going to fall off when I'm sleeping or showering?

"It's fine. It'll stay on. Just forget about it."

Okay, I say, still fingering the tiny, soft disk.

"I hope you don't mind my saying this. I heard you and Hen there on the phone. My two cents: It's probably best to keep this situation hush-hush, at least for now. You never know how others might react to your good fortune. There's not a lot of action or excitement around here. This is the kind of thing that could easily cause resentment. Jealousy is a common reaction in circumstances such as these. It's human nature."

It was only a thought, I say.

"Besides," he says, "keeping a secret is a kind of game. We're playing a game, okay? Think about it like that. Just a game. And games are meant to be fun."

T errance has given me some time alone, some time "to collect my thoughts." It feels like a few minutes, maybe fifteen, twenty, that I've been sitting in my chair, looking at the wall, attempting to focus. Thinking.

And then he's back at my side, smiling.

"Instead of my asking you so many questions about your work," he says, "I think I'll go there myself and have a look, maybe talk to a few of the workers there to get a feel for the locals."

I'm not keen on this idea. I don't want him digging around further into my life.

On a whim, I make a suggestion.

Why don't we go there together, we can do it now, I say.

"No, that's fine, Junior. I'd just feel bad making you leave the house with your shoulder like that."

I can still walk, I say. My legs are fine. And I know you want to see where I work, so might as well be now.

"Well, you're the boss," he says. "Okay then. Why not."

We walk outside together, get in opposite sides of my truck. Mill, I say, after turning the truck's engine on.

The navigation system blinks and beeps once in recognition.

"Is it sore?" he asks, once we pull out onto the road.

The shoulder?

"Yeah, just that the road might be bumpy. It isn't like resting at home in your chair."

It's okay, I say. Probably better to move around a bit. It's good to leave the house every once in a while. It's not healthy, physically or mentally, to never leave the house.

"How long have you had this truck?" he asks.

A while. It's not a new truck.

"It's in good shape."

Vehicles will last a long time if you treat them right.

"Like anything else," he says.

This is the first time I've been with Terrance outside the house. Sitting beside each other in the truck, I'm more aware of him than I have been previously. The truck is taking us to our destination, which gives me a chance to study him, like he does to me. His nails are bitten down; his wrists are thin. No beard or stubble to speak of. It would be easy to assume he's only around twenty-two, twenty-three. But he must be older to have the job he has. He must be at least thirty. He just doesn't look like it. It's the long hair, the baby face.

"So what's it like?"

The fields of tall yellow flowers rush by us.

What's what like? I ask.

"The mill. I'm curious," he says, turning toward me, pulling his left leg up under him. "I feel so comfortable with you, and with Henrietta, too, but I won't know anyone there. Tell me what to expect."

You ever been to a seed or grain mill before?

"No, I haven't."

It's really just a big building, I say. A few buildings. All connected.

I'm determined to turn the conversation back to him. I'm growing weary of this, of the focus on me all the time.

What kind of work have you done over the years? Before OuterMore, I ask.

"Whole bunch of different things. Took me a while to find what I was passionate about. To me, there has to be passion, otherwise why do it?"

I don't say anything to this. I'm not sure I would describe my feeling about the mill as passionate. It's a job. A job I'm good at. I need a job, so I work there. It's not like it's some ideal fantasy.

That's when he changes the subject. But I don't know why.

"Hen hasn't done much traveling, has she, or been away very much?"

No, she doesn't need any of that, I say. She's not a world traveler. She's quite content with her home and her lot in life. And there's nothing wrong with that.

"Of course not," he says. "Nothing at all. I heard her playing the piano last night. She's a beautiful player."

The best I know, I say.

I'm going to ask you something, I say. And I want an honest answer.

"Of course."

What's it like? This thing that will be here that's supposed to take my place? That's going to live with Hen.

There. It's the first time I've been so direct with him, the first time

I've brought it up. The replacement. I don't know why I do it now, but I suddenly felt an overwhelming urge to ask.

"It's not going to take your place, exactly, just hold it, like a substitute teacher coming in to teach a few classes, so the students don't fall behind."

Okay, I say.

But it's not okay. It's not okay with me at all.

"It's understandable that you're curious. Don't feel bad for asking."

I can't wrap my head around it, I go on. I've been trying, and I just can't.

"It'll look just like you, Junior. *Exactly* like you. So much so that not even you could tell the difference between yourself and it."

I look away from Terrance at my reflection in the window. There's no way a person can be so perfectly copied. It's not possible.

"If I were in your shoes, I'd feel the same disbelief. It goes back to earlier technology, just before you or I were born, around the time extensive 3D printing took off. The first feat was to 3D-print custom bones and joints for patients who needed replacements. This actually all started from health-care initiatives. These bones were manufactured but were not completely fake."

So not fully real, but also not entirely fake?

"You could say that, yes. They were made with calcium and other organic matter combined with synthetics. The technology just kept getting better. Then virtual reality as a leisure activity took off. What we do now is the natural progression from virtual reality. I don't think we realized how fast it would all happen, how fast VR would become obsolete, and where it would lead next."

I guess that's what always happens, I say. One thing paves the way for the next.

"Growth and advancement: it's human nature. It's always been this way. What's impossible becomes not only achievable but then is also quickly forgotten when the next impossibility becomes the new pursuit."

I guess we're the common thread, then.

"You mean humanity?"

Yeah, I say. I've been thinking more about this since you've arrived. About how we live. What we rely on. We depend on progress.

Terrance starts nodding. "Exactly. Even your truck. It wasn't that long ago, probably when your parents were kids, that people were still driving their own cars. It seems so stupid to us now, outrageous and dangerous that a fallible human would be controlling a massive hunk of metal moving at sixty miles an hour down a freeway, but for a few generations, that was the norm. Everyone owned cars, and people drove them themselves. No one thought twice about it."

And at the same time that everything changes, so much stays the same.

"Right. It's like the OuterMore slogan."

Go Farther, Be Better, I say.

He doesn't respond for a moment.

"You know our slogan?"

I guess so, I say. I must have seen it somewhere, or heard you mention it.

Terrance looks out his window. "I didn't realize how much of the land around here is canola fields," he says.

It's almost all been converted to canola. Look, I say. Up ahead. There it is.

It's the first break in the sea of yellow flowers since we've been driving, the mill's three towers.

"Huh. You're right, it's big," he says. "It looks old. Almost like it's abandoned."

It has seen better days, I say.

W e pull off the dirt road, drive through the mill's dilapidated chain-link gate into the gravel parking lot. I've been making this drive, from the house to this lot, for a long time. We find a spot at the end of a row of several trucks.

We'll go in the front door today, I say, but that's not normal for me. I usually go in through the back door, for workers.

Terrance takes out his screen, for notes or photos, I assume, or both.

A chime sounds as we enter; Terrance is a step or two behind me. There's no one around. Mary's not even here. Odd, I think. I was expecting to see her at her desk. She's the receptionist. She's usually here at this time of the day to greet people and answer any calls.

This way, I say.

I take him through the entrance, to the back, toward the first loading dock. There's no one in here, either.

"It's bigger than I pictured. Lots to see," Terrance says. "I'll probably have to come back again tomorrow for a bit, so I don't miss anything. Is the bathroom that way?" He asks, pointing to the long hall on our left.

Yeah, through there, at the end.

"I'll be right back."

I'm not often in this part of the mill. Never to stand here like this. It's particularly quiet today. Where is everyone? A single drip falls from the ceiling onto the floor beside my foot. There are a few drops collecting around a wet spot. The next drop is slow to form before falling, but does so, eventually.

Mary, I say, looking up to see her at the end of the hall. Hey, Mary.

She stops, looks at me.

"Junior. My god! How are you? I can't believe you're here." She starts walking toward me. "Look at you! Hen called. Told us about your shoulder. How are you feeling?"

Okay. Just little sore maybe. I'll be fine.

"What are you doing here?" she says. She pulls me in for a delicate hug. I have to lean down. She's careful around my shoulder. "I didn't think you could work, not so soon."

No, I can't right now. I'll be off for a bit.

Two of the guys walk by, both nod at Mary, but neither stops to talk.

"We'll miss you, of course. We have missed you. But we'll make do. You need to take all the time you need."

Was anyone asking about me today, wondering where I was?

"Today?" She swats dramatically at a fly that's buzzing around her head. "Oh, I'm not sure. Is there a reason why you came here today? You should be resting."

I was just dropping Terrance off, I say. He's having a look around.

A few hoppers have been turned on, and it's getting loud. It's getting harder to hear.

"Terrance?"

Yeah, Terrance. I have to yell now. Hen's . . . cousin. He's staying with us for a bit.

"Yes, that's right. Hen mentioned that. Well, it's nice to see you. I hope you start feeling like your old self soon," she says. "Remember: nothing's more important than your health."

W e were at the mill for about an hour. But here's an unsettling development I'm starting to become aware of, and one I assume that's been brought on by stress or lack of sleep: an hour used to feel like an hour, but lately, time has sped up. Or maybe it has slowed down.

How can perception change so fast in just a few days? Terrance looked around the loading docks on his own for a while, but when I was with him, he kept saying, "Look at this; look at that. And what do you think of this?" Asking me about the tools and equipment.

By the time we left, I was tense and irritated. He typed on his screen the entire drive home, while I looked out the window. He made one call, and it sounded like he was talking about me. I was hoping for some solitary time when we got home, but he wanted to talk again.

We're back in his makeshift interrogation studio. He's sitting behind me like last time. Hen was already home when we returned from the mill. I wanted to tell her about it, but Terrance was always in earshot, always getting between us.

"How are you feeling? How's the shoulder?" Terrance asks.

I don't really feel it, I say.

"Oh, really? No pain?"

No, no pain.

"Good, good. That's the pills. They're helping. Do you notice any dry mouth?"

I debate with myself what to tell him, how much to tell him.

I don't think so, but I've noticed, like, I've been feeling . . . mentally energized, like I've had too much coffee, but not jittery. Something else.

It's more than feeling energized. It's something deeper, but I don't tell him that.

"That's interesting," he says. "Glad to hear it."

But, it's strange, I say. I tried to think of something this morning, a memory of when I was a younger, sixteen and still in school, and I couldn't do it. I couldn't recall the details. I knew what the memory was supposed to be about, but that was all. Do you think what you're giving me might be affecting my memory?

Terrance looks at me seriously. "I'm not sure I understand. If you couldn't remember this memory of you at sixteen, how are you aware of it?"

That's the weird thing: I don't know. All I know is, I am aware of it. I know there's an important memory there, but it's just beyond my reach.

Hen appears at the door. I don't know how much she's heard.

"You can't be here," Terrance snaps when he sees her.

"Why are you asking him those questions? He's under a lot of stress, and you're not making him feel any better. You're making it worse."

"Hen, please. Now is not the time."

"It's not fair what you're doing."

Terrance raises his voice, which he's never done before. "I said that's enough! You have to leave us be."

Hey, I say, take it easy. She has just as much right to be here as we do!

"Junior, I need some one-on-one time with you without interruption. Hen, you're just making this worse. Please, I'm asking you nicely."

"You're doing fine, Junior, just answer his questions as best you can. I'll be downstairs."

She turns to leave without saying anything else to Terrance.

"You both have a lot on your mind," he says, "and I'm here getting in the way. I get it. But it is for the best. She'll be fine. I wouldn't worry about her reaction. I'm going to check a few things now, to be sure everything's okay. Blood pressure, heart rate, a few other things."

He stands, grabs a small device. He attaches something to my index finger. It starts beeping.

What's that? I ask.

"A monitor. No big thing."

He holds my other hand and spreads my index and middle fingers. He turns around, grabs something from a bag. He holds what looks like a small syringe. He takes my free hand again, and touches the syringe to the webbing between the fingers.

"You'll feel a quick prick," he says. "I'm just taking a sample."

I consider saying no, stopping him, but it happens so fast that I can't stop it. He inserts the thin point of the needle into the webbing between my fingers. I flinch, pulling my hand back reflexively.

Fuck!

"Sorry, it's done. I know, sensitive spot, right?"

He walks behind me but doesn't sit down.

"Can you lean forward for a moment?"

Like this?

I lean forward in my chair.

"Yeah, just rest your arms on your thighs. Yup, that's it."

I can feel his hands on my back, moving down my spine.

"Nice, that's good. Have you ever thought about traveling, Junior?"

Traveling? You mean the nice kind of traveling, that I get to choose on my own, instead of being forced to leave our atmosphere because of an imposed lottery?

He chuckles. "Exactly, yes."

No, not really.

"Don't you think it's a good idea to see other places beyond what you already know, even just to get out away from the farm for a few days, see some sites, expand your horizons?"

I've never considered it. It's never appealed to me. I've had responsibilities—work, home.

I like where I'm from, who I am. I'm comfortable here with Hen. I have a house and the chickens to look after.

"Well, what about Henrietta then? Has it ever occurred to you that she might want more than that?"

Like I said before, she loves it here. You should have seen what she came from, what her life was like before we got together.

"What was her life like before you guys got together? You mentioned in the car she didn't have a lot of money."

I feel a mild headache starting somewhere deep behind my eyes.

All I know is what she's told me, I say.

"And what is that?"

It wasn't good. She didn't have much where she was from. She grew up in a run-down farmhouse. They were dirt-poor.

"What do you know about her past?"

That's not what's important. I always knew I wanted to be with her. I knew we could be together and make it work. Her past was irrelevant to me.

"But you said that—"

Why are you asking about Hen? How does this matter? I ask, bringing a hand up to my temple.

"I need a full understanding of you. And what's more important than Hen?"

Nothing, I say. I think I'm done talking for now.

"It would be best if we stay up here a bit longer."

No, I don't want to talk to you anymore, I say, louder than intended.

"Is something wrong? Why are you rubbing your head like that?"

I hadn't realized I was still massaging my left temple. I stop when he mentions it.

Bit of a headache. I'd like to go downstairs now.

"Okay, okay. You're free to stop. You're not being held hostage. That's fine."

I get up, knocking over my chair, and storm down the narrow attic steps before he can say anything else.

My interview with Terrance was confusing, meandering, and disturbing, especially at the end when he started to ask about Hen so much. I know he would have pushed more had I not put a stop to it. I don't like that he's so interested in her. It makes me uneasy. Really, the whole formal-interview thing feels unnecessary. Can't he just hang around for a few days, watch how I live, listen to what I say, then get out? Wouldn't that suffice?

It's getting late. I should be tired, but I'm not. I've begun to develop a theory about Terrance. A theory about why he's really here, why he's asking these questions of his. I don't think he's being honest with me, with us. He's hiding something.

I walk to the kitchen, grab a beer. My mouth is dry, but I won't tell him that. It could be the pills, or the heat. The beer helps. I pace back and forth in front of the fridge for a few minutes, collecting my thoughts. I finish the beer. I open another. Hen's down in the cellar, playing the piano.

I'm careful as I creep slowly down the stairs. I make it all the way down. I keep my distance, standing behind her, sipping from my bottle, watching, listening. She's really something. She plays so well, smoothly. There's an undeniable fragility to her manner of playing. It reinforces my feeling of wanting to protect her, to be here for her, the way she was for me earlier. She came all the way to the attic to see if I was okay. She defended me. What would I be without her? It's a scary reflection, and I put it out of my mind. I recognize the song she's playing. I like when I recognize it. I enjoy it more. It's one she used to play some time ago but hasn't played much recently.

I take another long, greedy swig. The beer is helping my head. I watch her.

Maybe I'm not as average as I've always believed. It's a heavy thought, bracing. I've never considered this before. It must be the combination of the beer, my talk with Terrance, and Hen's playing this particular song.

I take another few steps closer, so I'm now right behind her. She still doesn't know I'm here. She has yet to miss a note. She doesn't delay or pause. There are no mistakes or miscues. It's amazing. She's amazing.

Things are getting clearer. It's not because of the lottery or Outer-More. I'm reflecting on things, taking stock, evaluating what I have with new eyes, thinking about my life in a different way.

I finish my beer. I set the bottle down softly at my feet and take yet another step toward her. I'm not in a hurry. Now I'm right behind her. I reach out and put a hand on her shoulder. She flinches in surprise, striking the wrong key. She stops playing, resting her hands in her lap.

Keep going, I say. It's beautiful. You play so well.

"You scared me," she says.

I just wanted to see you. I want to be with you. I've barely seen you all day.

I can feel the dampness, the sweat on her skin.

"It's been another weird day in a series of weird days," she says. "Still no rain. I'm starting to worry."

I don't want you to worry. Not ever.

"I know you don't. I know. Do you like when I play?"

Yes, I do. You play so well.

She turns around on the bench so she's facing me. "I'm going to tell you something: It's not really for me. Did you know that? I don't play for myself. I play because . . . because you want me to. I play for you."

What she's just told me is significant, but I sense she's not done, that she's going to keep talking, that she wants to say more.

Go on, I say.

"You like my playing. And like so many things, you think it's good for me, but it isn't. It doesn't help me feel better. I don't even like sitting down here. And you can be completely oblivious about this kind of thing, whether you realize it or not. There are so many instances when I've expected you to understand how I'm feeling, and it just doesn't happen. It's so discouraging, draining. It's like as long as we're here, moving from day to day, you're convinced that I'm happy. Honestly, I rarely feel happy. And I don't want to have to tell you everything. I shouldn't have to. Not if you're paying attention, even just a bit, considering me in a way that's not just superficial. I want my own identity separate from being your wife. It's just how it should be."

Her voice is smooth, not rising or shaking. Her tone is steady, thoughtful, composed, sober.

So this is something I've been doing? I ask. It's something I'm doing that's making you feel this way?

"It's more something you haven't been doing."

I'm listening, I say. I'm glad you're being honest, but what you're saying isn't good. I don't like that you're feeling like this. You haven't talked about any of this before.

"No, I couldn't. But these last couple of years, ever since Terrance first showed up, I may not have been talking much, but I've been thinking a lot. Thinking about us. Having these talks with you is the first step to figuring out . . . what I need to figure out."

You can always talk to me, Hen. Anytime, I say.

"Thank you," she says.

I mean it, I say.

She puts a hand on my arm.

"What if it never comes?" she says. "The storm. The rain. We act like it has to come, like it's inevitable because it has always come before, but what if a storm doesn't come this time and things just keep going on and on like this forever? What then? I'm not sure I can keep going on and on like this, even though I'm supposed to. I don't think I can."

Before I can reply, or say anything else, she stands, pushes the bench back with her legs, and walks upstairs without another word.

A lone again. Thankfully. I need more time to think. In the living room, sitting in the chair, my chair, in the dark. I'm getting used to my daily and nightly solitude.

For a while I listened to Hen and Terrance walking around above me, taking turns in the bathroom, tap running, toilet flushing, talking in the hall, getting ready for bed. They've been chatting a lot, but not formally the way I do in the interviews I've had with Terrance. Now they're in their beds, asleep.

My shoulder is feeling better. Terrance gave me another dose of pills. I've decided tomorrow is going to be a big day. Terrance isn't being completely honest with me, and I intend to figure out what he's concealing. How can I be on the verge of discovery when I don't even know what I'm looking for?

I don't feel like sleep will come, not yet. I'm not tired. I'm alert.

My eyes have adjusted to the darkness. I close my eyes, open them, close them, open them. Open. Closed. Open. Closed.

When I can't sleep, it's Hen I think about. I often think back to when we found her piano. We didn't find it until we'd been living in the house for a few days. The previous owners had left it down in the cellar, hidden under a dusty blanket. A piano. It was in terrible shape. I have no idea how it got down there or why it was put there. Someone likely considered it garbage and couldn't be bothered to move it.

I was excited when I saw it. I knew Hen had played the piano at school when she was a child. I figured she'd love to start playing again. It was another sign that we'd made the right decision in buying the house we had. When I told her what I'd found, she didn't share my enthusiasm. It was disappointing.

You don't seem overly interested, I said, after leading her down blindfolded and removing the blanket.

"It's cool," she said. "But I don't really play anymore."

But now you can, I said.

"I guess I could. It's not in great shape. And it's all the way down in the cellar."

I'm sorry the free piano isn't brand-new, Hen. But it's yours, and you're going to love it.

I cleaned the piano up for her, but we could never properly tune it. Hen tried for a while and then gave up.

We'll get used to it, I told her. Slightly discordant isn't the worst thing in the world.

"Good. You're awake," says Terrance. "I was trying to be quiet, but I couldn't hold out forever."

It's fine, I say. I have to get up. What time is it?

I smell cooking, spices, can hear a pan sizzling.

"Almost nine, sleepyhead," he says. "You were dead to the world. I would have waited, but . . . Here, you're overdue."

He has a tea towel slung over his shoulder. He holds his hand out to me. Three white pills lie in his palm.

Three?

"Same pills as yesterday. For the pain."

It occurs to me that I don't need them anymore.

I'm not in a lot of pain, I say.

I take them in my hand, delaying, considering. He waits. I pop them in my mouth. They taste vaguely of rubber.

"That's a good, long sleep you had. I'm so pleased. It's exactly what you needed."

I move the thin sheet I've been using off me and swing my legs over the side of the chair so both my feet are on the floor.

Yeah, I say. I don't know if I really slept all that much

"I think you're getting used to the chair. I don't know if I would. I sometimes can't even sleep in a comfortable bed."

I yawn, rubbing my forehead, trying to wake up. My head, the same spot as yesterday, is feeling a bit sore again this morning.

I don't remember falling asleep, I say.

"I hope you don't mind. I was up, thought I'd get going on some breakfast."

I look over toward the kitchen, trying to steady my gaze, focusing on Terrance. He's standing by the oven, talking over his shoulder. Where's Hen? I get up, walk into the kitchen. The carton of eggs is open on the counter. So are the cutting board, my chef's knife, and a silver bowl. My cast-iron pan is on one of the elements. Scrambled eggs? He's wearing my apron.

"I hope I made enough."

We usually don't have much of a breakfast, I say. Where's Hen?

"Not sure where she's at. Breakfast is one meal that everyone should always eat. I've been thinking: you need to be eating more, keep your strength up. Have you lost weight? Breakfast sets you up. Fuel for the day! Gets the metabolism going. You'll be eating a regulated breakfast on the trip. Three balanced meals for everyone. What do you do with your eggshells?"

The smell of the food cooking is off-putting. He's put something unusual in the eggs.

What do you have in there?

"I jazzed them up a bit. Spices. Eggs are pretty bland on their own."

I open a drawer and take out the bag of coffee and a filter.

"Sorry, I should have put the coffee on first. I should know better by now."

Are you having some? I ask.

"No coffee for me, thanks."

Terrance starts whistling as he moves the cooking eggs around with a wooden spoon. I'm pouring the water into the back of the coffee machine when Hen walks in.

"Terrance is making breakfast?" she says.

"I'm happy to. I never like to miss breakfast, and I've been up for a while."

Where have you been? I ask Hen.

"Went out for a walk. I was awake early."

"Are you hungry?" he says to her.

"Yeah, I am. Morning," she says, touching my arm as she walks past me to the sink.

Coffee?

"I'm okay. I think I'll wait until I get to work," she says.

Really? You always have a cup here before you leave.

"I'm trying to cut back. I want to make a few changes."

One cup here and one at work isn't going to kill you.

"No, I know. But I'm okay."

She bumps into Terrance by the fridge. Says sorry. He touches her back. There's not much room between the oven and the fridge.

"This is ready."

"I'll get the plates," says Hen. "Smells good. What did you put in there?"

"A few extras. Hopefully it works. I just made it up with what you had. Eating is always more pleasurable after vigorous exercise."

I'm still in the shorts I slept in. No shirt. I'm not hungry. My stomach is in a knot. My head's not clearing yet.

I'm just going to have some coffee, I say.

"You sure?" says Terrance. "I made the breakfast for you, mostly. I really think you should."

"He's already made the food," says Hen, setting three plates around the table. "You probably should eat."

I'm not hungry yet, and I don't feel like sitting again right away. I've been sitting all night. I'm not a five-year-old kid.

My tone is sharp, but I don't care. They look at each other, then at me. These increasing liberties he's taking are an overstep, and I won't accept it. He's a stranger. A stranger in my home.

"No problem," says Terrance. "Your choice."

Terrance carries the pan over to the table. He doles out two helpings until the pan is empty, leaving the dried-on bits. He sets the dirty pan back down on the stove.

"Hope it tastes okay," he says.

"Looks amazing," Hen says.

The coffee isn't finished percolating, but I interrupt the process, remove the carafe, and take a cup. I have my back to the table but can hear them eating, cutlery on plates, chewing.

"Actually, it's delicious," says Hen. "My god, really."

"Not too spicy?"

"No, not at all. I love it."

I turn around, resting my lower back against the counter.

I want him away from her.

Ready to go in about ten minutes? I say to Terrance.

"I was thinking I could drop him off at the mill," says Hen. "You took him yesterday. You don't need to go anywhere today."

The mill's the wrong direction for you. You'd have to head the wrong way.

"There's no point in your leaving the house when you're trying to rest."

I take a sip of the coffee. Hot coffee. Hot coffee on another hot morning. He could just take his own car. But I'm sure he'd say that would be missing an opportunity to talk with Hen. That's when I see it on the counter, to the right of the coffeemaker.

A horned beetle. Just sitting there, motionless. Looking at me.

"Are you sure?" Terrance asks. "I don't want to put you out."

Neither Terrance nor Hen has seen it. I'm glad they haven't. They'd just want to kill it right away.

"You have stuff to do around here, don't you, Junior?" Hen says. "Junior?"

Yeah, I say. I have some work planned around here.

"I'll pick Terrance up at the mill when I'm done at work," says Hen.

That'll be a few hours, won't it?

"That'll be fine," he says.

Terrance is finished with his plate. He stands and carries it over to the sink.

"Most people don't get this chance. They don't appreciate what you are now appreciating, and that means not taking your days for granted. Enjoy the feeling. And before I forget, I noticed the shower is dripping a bit. I turned it off when I was done and the drip wouldn't stop. Nothing serious, but wanted to let you know."

Another sip of coffee.

I'll take a look, I say.

"That was really good. Just leave your plate," says Hen. "Junior's not going anywhere today. He can clean up."

I have to do more for Hen. I picked up on it this morning, her reticence and shifting moods. I haven't been doing enough. I need to show her I care, that I'm aware and concerned. I need to impress her before I leave.

It doesn't take long to clean up from breakfast, apart from having to scrub the skillet in hot water with steel wool for about ten minutes. It would have been a much quicker task had Terrance just left the pan to soak instead of putting it back on the stove. It's not the end of the world, but it's annoying.

My shoulder is tender when I finish. I have a busy day planned. I have lots to do around here. My time is running out. My days left are fewer. I can feel it in my bones. An urgency. There aren't enough hours in the day anymore. There never were, but there are even fewer now. It's sad, but also unexpectedly thrilling.

I need to be productive today, despite my injury. It's just my shoulder. I don't want Hen worrying about things when I'm gone. My to-do list is never-ending. In the past, that's made me more inclined to put the work off. Where would I start? But now that I know I'm leaving, I've felt a greater need to achieve. Now. Today. I have responsibilities, duties, chores. What would life be without them? Easier, but in no way satisfying. We need to be engaged and challenged. We all need to be productive and produce.

Some of the work is obvious. It would be clear to anyone. The posts on the stairs need to be repainted. The old wallpaper in the living room is peeling near the top of the wall. There are yellow and brown stains on a few of the ceilings. The carpet under the couch and chairs is frayed and ratty. None of the tasks are overwhelming. No big projects. There's plenty of it, but it's all small stuff.

The shower is also dripping, so I've been told. As Terrance said, there is always a positive way to look at things, an opportunity to acknowledge and prioritize.

Most people don't get this chance, he said. *They don't appreciate what you are now appreciating, and that means not taking your days for granted. Enjoy the feeling.*

I've been getting the impression that Terrance thinks my house is in bad shape, that he's silently judging us. Judging me. He hasn't come out and said that, not directly. He's made a few comments. It's more the way he looks when he sees some chipped paint or a crack in a window.

I'm not going to make decisions because Terrance doesn't approve.

I wonder what his house is like. I have no idea. I'm sure if I was living there, I could find a few things wrong with it, some dirt under the rug.

I'll do what I want. What I think is important. I already have a plan in my head. I'm in control.

Everything is old in here, I know. It's my house. It's my stuff. At least, I think it's mine. Lately I've been puzzling over this. Some of these things—the furniture, the dishes in the kitchen—don't feel as recognizable as they should. I eat off these dishes every day, but they don't tell a story, not the way some of our stuff does, and yet I know they're ours. Still, I feel no special attachment to them. Another unintended symptom, I guess, of the stress of this whole scenario.

With the pan finally clean, I leave everything to dry in the rack. I turn off the tap. Without the running water, it's quiet now.

I walk upstairs to our bedroom and sit down on our bed. Hen left it unmade, disheveled. I miss being in here at night. I miss sleeping in my bed with my wife. I head down the hall to the bathroom. I stand in front of the mirror. I correct my posture, straightening my shoulders. I turn to the side, then back to the front. I open my mouth as wide as possible. I yell. I yell again, louder, as loud as I can.

I lift my right arm up, flex it. I'm strong, but I could be in better shape. It hasn't been a concern of mine, not for years. It wouldn't take much to tone up. I just need to alter my routine a bit, maybe include a few exercises that would be suitable for my shoulder. I can't do push-ups or pull-ups right now. But I could probably do some sit-ups, some squats. There's no reason I can't do this. It's in me to make changes. Self-improvement.

I bring my hand up, behind my head. I touch the censor that Terrance put there. It feels larger, as if it's growing, but that's impossible, I know. I wonder if the sensor is picking up my improved health. It feels warmer than it did when he first put it on me, almost like it's glowing.

I do one squat. And then another. I continue—fifteen, sixteen, seventeen—until my legs are burning. I'm pleased that I'm able to do the squats without any pain to my shoulder. My torso is shaking on the last two, but I complete them. I wait for a few minutes, resting. I do twenty more. And then another fifteen. I'm dripping with sweat and I'm panting. I'm happy with these results.

I return to the kitchen. The beetle hasn't moved, not an inch. It's just sitting there on the counter. I know because I've been watching it. My heart is grinding away in my chest, pumping, almost bursting from the exercise. I like how it feels right now, beating this hard, working and working, all on its own.

What constitutes normalcy? I think if you asked fifty people, you'd get fifty different answers. There would, undoubtedly, be some congruities. But who decides what's normal? Where does the line of regularity fall? I have time to consider this type of metaphysical conundrum now because I'm here in my house all alone. I have the time, space, and a renewed mental vigor.

I've always felt it about myself, going back as far as the memory of when I first met Hen, that day on the road, even then—a profound burden of mediocrity. But I'm sensing a change. I'm here after all! Right now! I'm having experiences, feeling desires, making decisions, building relationships, creating new memories. And I'm aware of them all happening at once. How can any of this be standard and typical?

I always thought I was ordinary, but that is my own illusion, it seems. Ordinary is impossible. It's more realistic to believe that we are all exceptional, that I, too, am singular, unique, that there has never been nor ever will be another me.

I'm an individual. I'm unprecedented and unimaginable. I'm impossible. Me, right now, standing in my house, considering my uncertain future, reflecting on my own experiences.

But what about Hen? Before I met her? Who was I then?

"Junior?"

"Hey, Junior?"

"Junior, what are you doing?"

I turn around. Hen and Terrance are back from work. Already? They're standing in the kitchen looking at me. When did they arrive? I didn't hear the car or the front door.

Hey, I say, you guys just get back?

"What are you doing?"

"You were just standing there," says Terrance. "Looking at the counter. Are you all right?"

Fine, I say.

Maybe it is actually later than I thought. I must have lost track of time, which happens when you're thinking and functioning and understanding on a new level. I've used my day effectively, to improve, and that's a good feeling. I'm happy with myself and what I've accomplished in a single afternoon.

"My forearms are on fire," he says. "You weren't kidding, Junior. That's hard work you do at the mill."

He's retying his ponytail, pulling it tight.

You weren't really working, were you? Were you . . . doing my job?

"They could probably use the help," says Hen. "You know how it gets there when they're short people."

"Yeah," says Terrance, "because you're out injured, and they haven't filled those hours. I was looking around a bit, but then they said they could use my help. I pitched in a little."

I don't think he's physically cut out for my job. He wouldn't last. Not for long.

What did they have you doing, exactly? I ask.

"I had to hold those white bags as they filled up with seed or grain and stack them."

Huh, I say.

Hen has been putting away the dishes I washed, but then she stops suddenly. She leaves the room without saying anything. I hear her going up the stairs.

So you did my work, I say, the bagging.

"And they asked if I would come back tomorrow, to fill in for you."

They did? I say.

I feel my face redden.

Hen calls me from upstairs, asking if I can come up there, give her a hand with something.

Give me a second, I say to Terrance.

It takes me longer than it used to to get up the stairs. It's not only my shoulder but my legs. They're tired from my exercises this morning. I have to hold the bannister with my good arm and go up carefully, one step at a time. When I get to our room, I feel out of breath. Hen is standing by the window, looking out. She hears me and turns my way.

You all right? I ask.

"Fine. I just wanted to make sure *you* were all right. I was worried it might be awkward down there, just the two of you. Again. I'm feeling uncomfortable about him being here today."

It's okay, I say.

"I'm not sure it is."

What do you mean?

"He's going to be up here any minute, interrupting us."

Say what you have to say.

"What's he asking you about now?"

He's telling me about his day. They had him bagging at the mill for some reason.

"But he probably hasn't told you everything."

What do you mean?

"I couldn't say anything to you this morning, but I took him to the mill so he could talk to me. I'm worried about you." She steps away from the window and lowers her voice. "I'm feeling bad about what's happening here. I haven't said everything that I could have. I'm not supposed to. He might be listening to us right now, but it's not fair to you."

I've been feeling pretty great, I say.

"You don't get it. Didn't you hear what I just said? You don't have to sit and talk to him all the time. That's not right. That's not what this is supposed to be about."

Is that what I'm doing? Am I just doing what he tells me to do?

Isn't that why he's here, I say, to gather information, for your sake and for mine? And actually, I have more energy than usual. I feel spry and sturdy, I feel . . .

I move closer, putting my hand on her hip. She pivots, turns to face the window again.

I don't know what you want from me. I can't just get up and go lie down and rest when I feel like, not as easily as you. I have responsibilities. I'm the one leaving. I have a lot to do before I go.

"Just forget it," she says. "I don't know why I bothered calling you up here. Forget it."

I'm going to go back down then, if that's all.

"Fine. Go. Get out. And close the door behind you."

B ack to the kitchen, newly irritated and puzzled.

What's wrong with her? What was she talking about? I hate when Hen gets like this. When she's upset, but evasive. Whatever is wrong, she always wants me to pry it out of her, which makes everything harder and worse. It's brutal behavior. Childish. She needs to grow up. Where do these moods come from? They've developed over time like most bad habits.

Terrance is seated at the table. A paper napkin has been ripped into thin strands. He pushes it aside when I sit down. I can tell he's been listening to us arguing upstairs. He's trying to hide it, act like he was just on his screen, busy with something else, but I can tell.

"Everything okay?" he asks.

Fine, I say.

"You sure?"

Yes. So what were you saying? You were saying something when I left. About the mill.

"I was going to ask what you think of it when you're there but not working."

I'm always working at the mill. That's what I'm there for.

"But I mean during the downtime. Like on break, or at lunch. Do you use the lunchroom?"

No, I say. Not really. I stick to myself mostly.

"And why's that?" Terrance asks.

It's easier than making small talk.

"What about eating? Do you eat alone, too?"

Yeah, usually.

"And why's that? Any particular reason?

People can be disgusting, I say.

He picks up his screen, turns something on, maybe a recorder.

"How so?" he asks.

I got in the habit of looking at the guys in the lunchroom. Watching them bite hunks of their sandwiches. The bread and filling being ground together into some vile paste. Whatever wasn't swallowed would end up stuck between beige teeth and infected gums. Sorry, but it's true. It's not just eating. I've seen a coworker fall asleep during a break with his mouth gaping open. I felt sick at the sight of it. We're oblivious to it most of the time. And one day, I started to think about why that is, as I watched one of the guys wipe his mouth on his napkin after eating and then blow his snotty nose into the same napkin, which he then balled up and dropped onto his plate, and very slowly the napkin started to unfold from the ball all on its own, as if it wanted to be seen, and that's when I realized our common seam, each of us, is our own inherent vulgarity. Think about earwax, and fingernails, and pus. I've seen guys spit on the ground and walk away. And we do all this stuff automatically.

I take a breath and see Terrance completely focused on me. "You've never mentioned any of this before, at least not to me," he says.

It's not like I spend my life sitting around obsessing over this, I say. I'm just . . . aware of it. At work, especially, it's all around.

Terrance begins typing something into his screen.

I'm tired, I say. I think I should get ready for bed.

He's interviewing her now. Hen and Terrance are talking about who knows what. Unlike with me, he didn't take her up to the attic. They're just sitting in the kitchen. I'm in the living room. It sounds more casual and laid-back than our interviews.

I thought I might be able to fall asleep early, but there's no way now. I get up from my chair and walk toward their voices. I stand in the hall outside the kitchen. I listen. They're speaking quietly because they know I'm close by and I told them I was going to try to sleep.

I'd like to be able to see Hen and Terrance talking, see where they're sitting, how they're positioned at the table, but they would stop the conversation if I entered the kitchen. They want to be alone. Terrance is always trying to be alone with Hen.

"But do any of us really have the freedom we think we have?" she asks.

"I would say so, yes," Terrance replies.

"Think about all the different forces and pressures that play a role in shaping what we do, how we act, how we dress, what we think. It's hard, maybe impossible, not to be influenced by that."

"We know what we're doing, though," he says. "We can either accept or reject those forces."

I put a hand up to my eye because I feel it twitching. I apply light pressure.

"You know what everyone has been telling me my whole life? That this is where I'm from and this is what I know and this is what I like and I'm lucky to have what I have. And he's always said that I would hate the city, that I would be uncomfortable and scared. Is that actually true? Or is it just what I've been told over and over?"

Terrance makes a sound of acknowledgment, an inquiring hum.

"I have this fantasy," Hen continues. "A fantasy about finding out for myself and making the decision that I'm done. That I can't do it anymore. That I want something else. Something for me. If I decide to leave, you know?"

Leave? What does she mean by that? She's not the one leaving. I am. There's nowhere for Hen to go. My hand is still pressed against my twitching eye, and I'm listening intently.

"What would that take?" he asks.

"For me to leave?"

"Yes."

"It would take my finding the courage to do something drastic and permanent. And my fantasy is that instead of trying to explain it, to list my reasons, to rationalize and justify, I would do the opposite."

"What's the opposite of justifying it?" asks Terrance.

"I would just go. I wouldn't spell it out. Not explaining myself is more powerful. Why should the onus be on me to explain myself?

It should be on him to try to figure out what happened. I would still leave a note, though. A note with his name on it. But it would be blank. There would be nothing there. It would say nothing and everything at the same time. What could be more explicit than that?"

Terrance says something that I can't hear. I step around the corner. Terrance is startled when he sees me. He stops what he's about to say and stares. Hen's wearing her black tank top, sitting in her normal spot at the kitchen table. Terrance is in my spot, beside her. He's wearing my apron again.

"Junior," he says. "I thought you were sleeping."

No, I'm not tired yet, I say.

"You hungry? I made some food."

Terrance stands up. I wonder what's the worst thing that's ever happened to Terrance? What's his biggest regret? What's the greatest shame he's experienced? What's the most pain he's felt?

He steps toward me. He looks into my eyes.

"You're looking a bit flushed," he says.

He feels both sides of my neck, my glands. I flinch as he does it, not expecting him to get so close, to touch me. He takes an instrument of some kind out of his back pocket. He holds it up to me.

"Sorry, just want to take your temperature. Won't take a second."

He inserts the device into my ear before I can protest.

He takes it out, looks at it.

"Good. Nothing to worry about. You're sure you're feeling okay?"

Yeah, better than ever.

"Excellent."

He puts his hand on my chest, presses it against my skin. He holds it there.

"Your heart feels good, too," he says. "Strong."

He's never touched me like this before. I'm taken aback.

"Will you please eat something? I'm still a bit concerned about your weight."

Not just yet, I say. Maybe later, if I get up in the night. I've been waking up.

"I'll make something tasty tomorrow. Hen, we can shop for some groceries when your shift is done. I'll probably finish around the same time tomorrow."

"Sure, yeah," she says, but she's looking at me.

Hen hates grocery shopping.

You're really going back to the mill again tomorrow?

"Yes. I am," he says. "And then Hen and I will pick up groceries."

I can't believe I didn't notice before. Not until right now. It hits me like a slap. I see what he's trying to do. I see where this is going. I was developing a theory, but now I know for sure. I see why he's here, living with us, observing, asking so many questions. It makes so much more sense than what he's been telling us all along. He's been lying to me, to us, this entire time.

It's him. It's Terrance. He's the one. He's the one who is going to be staying here, living here with my wife when I'm gone. That's what he wants.

It's him. Terrance is going to be my replacement.

Terrance has gone up to his room. Hen and I are alone in the kitchen. Now is the moment I can tell her what's really going on. But I have to be careful. I don't want to worry her or make her anxious.

So did you two have a good talk? Was it interesting? Did you connect?

"I'm tired," she says.

Why do you think he's so insistent to take you shopping? I ask. To drive to work with you? To be with you all the time?

She shakes her head slowly. She really is tired. I can see it in the rounded slump of her shoulders. "How would I know why he does anything? Please, don't push me on this."

Isn't it strange how much he wants to help out here? He's not our guest.

"Yes, he is."

You're the one who told me to be more aware and assertive and not do everything he tells me to. We never invited him. We don't know him.

"He wants to do a nice thing, I guess."

You think he just wants to do a nice thing? You don't believe that. I can tell by the way you said it.

"It's possible he's showing off a bit, trying to impress."

Showing off? Because he can take you grocery shopping?

Hen rubs her eyes. She's exasperated. "Look. What do you think is going on?"

I'm afraid to say it outright. I'm not ready to tell her yet, about Terrance, and the real reason he's here.

I just think it's a weird thing to want to take someone's wife to the grocery store, spend all your time with her. Will you go?

"I already said I would. You're making a big deal of this, Junior."

Do you think he's telling us the truth? I ask. About everything?

She runs her hand through her hair. "As much as he can, yes."

So you agree there might be something he's keeping from us? Something he's not telling us?

"I wish you would stop worrying so much about him. You're getting too worked up."

I'm not getting worked up, I say. I'm starting to understand.

"Hold your arms up, like this," Terrance says, stretching his arms up over his head to demonstrate. I left Hen sitting at the kitchen table. Terrance called me upstairs, and I'm back in the sweltering attic. I want to question his demand, tell him no, resist, but again, pathetically, I have complied and done as he asked.

"I have a couple more tiny sensors to put on you."

Why?

"The more data we—"

Yes, yes, always more data, I say. Is this all for the replacement?

"This is all for Hen, Junior. Remember that. We want the replacement to be as authentic and real as possible. Yeah, right here," he says, pressing a sensor into my left armpit. "And, yup, another here."

He puts another in my right armpit. This one pinches and I flinch.

Shit, I say.

"Oh, sorry. It's done. You're good," he says. "Have a seat. Are you feeling good, relaxed, composed?"

It's late, later than any other interview we've had.

I can't see anything in the room, I say. It's unsettling.

"Just close your eyes, if you'd prefer."

Terrance walks behind me. I hear him sit down in his chair.

"It's better like this. You just focus ahead of you. How do you feel?"

Good, clearheaded, I say. Strong, productive. I have a focus. I know things now.

He types something into his screen.

I've been thinking, I say. I don't know how this'll work. I've been feeling different lately, unique.

"Interesting. You felt ordinary before, I take it. What's this change about, in your opinion?"

Me, I say. It's about me.

It's about you, too, I think. But I don't reveal that. Not yet.

I've become more aware of myself. Because of the situation. Now that I know I'm leaving, I see things differently. I've been aware of little things that I would have missed before.

"Like what?"

Like seeing the sun shine off the roof of our old barn. I saw that this morning and stood there, looking at it. I found it moving. It was beautiful—it really was. I don't usually think about if a landscape is beautiful or not, but I couldn't control this feeling. I saw it and recognized that it was beautiful. But you know what? It made me sad.

"Sad?" I can hear him typing. He's trying to do it quietly, but I can hear. "Why?"

I don't know. I have no idea.

"Because beauty is fleeting, maybe?"

No, I say. It's the opposite. Beauty isn't fleeting. Beauty is eternal. But . . . I'm not. I'm fleeting. That's more the point.

His typing stops abruptly.

"That's quite profound. You do seem more self-aware and introspective than when I first arrived. It makes me think of Baudelaire: 'I can barely conceive of a type of beauty in which there is no melancholy.'"

I decide to say it then, to get closer to what I know to be true.

I can't be replaced, I say. Not really. Whatever it is, no matter how much it looks like me, sounds like me. Whatever it is, it won't be me.

"There's nothing wrong with self-confidence, Junior, self-belief. It's healthy. We encourage it. It doesn't impact our initiative."

This isn't self-belief or confidence. It's an awakening, a new alertness, a knowing. I'm not like others. I've always thought I was, but I'm not. You can't replicate me. I didn't understand this until—

"Actually, Junior. Sorry, not to cut you off, but I was hoping tonight's chat would focus a bit more on you *and* Henrietta. How are you guys doing, as a couple? I've been—and I hope I'm not speaking out of place here—but I've been noticing some slight tension, perhaps?"

I sit up straighter in my seat.

Between us?

"Yeah. I'm curious, that's all. With everything that's been happening. Have you guys been talking a lot? I could be wrong, of course, but what's the mood like between you two? It doesn't seem like you talk or even spend much time together these days."

You are wrong. The mood is good. It's fine. We're fine, I say. It's my responsibility to make sure we're okay. It's on me.

"That's good. I don't mind being wrong about that. Has she been sleeping well?"

As far as I know.

I don't enjoy this. I don't like his asking about Hen.

"Good. It's just, do you guys share everything? Do you always know what's happening with her, how she's feeling?"

Why?

Terrance has started typing again; I can hear him tapping away at his screen.

Why are you asking that question?

"I'm interested in your relationship and how you two interact and communicate. So much of a relationship depends on open and honest communication. I want you to tell me specifically about Hen."

I can't help it. My heart rate has increased again.

I want to ask him what's going on, demand that he tell me. Tell him to leave my home. Tell him he has no right to be here.

"Does she tell you what she likes?"

Who?

"Your wife, Junior."

You mean to eat?

"No, not to eat." He laughs. "What her preferences are, you know, in bed? Does she tell you, or do you just do what she likes intuitively?"

I wipe some sweat from my head and neck.

What did you say?

"Junior. Don't get so uptight. I'm just curious."

That's private. You have no right to ask that. That's between me and Hen. What makes you think you can ask me that question? What makes you think you're—

"Okay, okay. Relax," he says brusquely. "I have something to put on your wrist. On your good arm."

What? What is it?

"It helps moderate hydration. We can't let you get dehydrated. Hold out your hand, like this."

He demonstrates with his own arm, holding it parallel to the floor.

"Come on," he says. "Now."

He brings up a metal clasp and fastens it around my wrist. It's tight. There's a single loop on one side, where something else could be attached.

"There, that's it," he says. "You're free to go."

I look at the clamp, shining and new. It's never been used. The metal is cold. For some reason I can't explain, it feels good.

I need a shower, badly. I'm greasy and disheveled. I've never felt so angered, so disrespected.

This feeling has been growing since Terrance entered our lives, and it's become a constant concern since Hen suggested I didn't have to do everything this man said. Why am I allowing him to control me? I'm still in my house. I haven't gone anywhere yet. I should have seen this before. Now it's all I can see. Hen has been trying to tell me something. I know that. I know there's more she wants to tell me, but she won't. Or she can't. I'm understanding more and more every day. Every hour. Every minute.

This is all for Hen, Junior. Remember that. We want the replacement to be as authentic and real as possible, he said.

The sweat is pouring off me. I'm standing in the bathroom, trying to collect my thoughts and understand what's happening, and what I can do, what actions I can take. I'm not sure we should spend another night in this house with Terrance. He's a threat. He's our enemy.

But if we did leave, then what? Would he follow us? Probably, yes. He would follow us just as I was followed that day that I went out to the field and found that burning barn. He would find us. They would find us. OuterMore. Whatever it is. No, we can't leave. That would only make things worse.

Does she tell you what she likes? he said.

I need to think. Or I need to stop thinking. I'm not sure which is best. I want to forget about the interviews. Forget about Terrance. Try to sleep. Reassess in the morning. I turn on the shower, the hot water, and take off the few clothes I'm wearing.

I don't get in right away. I stand naked in front of the mirror. I raise my good arm up above my head. I flex my biceps. I hold the pose, straining. I flex my abs as tight as I can. I turn from side to side, examining my obliques.

You're free to go, he said.

I wipe the condensation that's fogged up the glass. My face is now only a few inches from the mirror. I flare my nostrils. I open my eyes as wide as they'll go. I'm a flawed, disgusting person like everyone else. Broken and imperfect. Of course I am. How could I ever think I was any different?

I hold my eyes wide until they start to hurt. I hold them like that longer. I hold them like that until my eyes start to tear up.

Terrance wants to know too much. He wants to know everything about me. He will never know everything about me. I've been good to Hen. What would her life have been like if we'd never met? I could have had others if that's what I wanted. I don't care if we fight. This is her life. This is where she lives. With me. Clearly, she's chosen this life. She's chosen me. Which means she is happy. The way things are.

The mirror has fogged up again. I use my index finger to draw a picture of a beetle in the condensation. I do it slowly, my hand squeaking against the wet surface. I know what Terrance is planning when he sends me away to the Installation, when he takes over my life. He wants to move from the guest room down the hall into my bedroom. He wants to know me so he can be me. But that will never happen. He'll never be me.

I step into the shower. I hold my face up to the water.

Even with the shower on, I can hear talking from Terrance's room. His room is right next door. It's Hen. She's in there now with him. I can't decipher what they're talking about. I move closer to the tiled wall, but still can't hear any better. What are they talking about? I turn the hot water on more, until it's nearly scorching. It's me. I'm sure they're talking about me. They're obsessed with me.

When I can't take it any longer, I turn off the shower and step out onto the mat to dry. I'm being careful while drying my bad shoulder. My bad shoulder. The reason I can't sleep in my own bed with Hen. The reason I have to sleep sitting up, alone, downstairs. The reason why it's so easy for Terrance to step in, to get closer and closer to Hen.

I turn around in front of the mirror so I can inspect my shoulder. I don't know why, but I've never looked at it since the accident. Why did it never occur to me to examine it? There's a dressing on it, the same one that's been on there since the accident. It hasn't been changed.

I pick at the tape holding the dressing on. I slowly lift it. I take my time, removing all four pieces of tape. I let the dressing fall to the floor. I run my hand over the skin underneath. The smooth skin. There's no scar on my shoulder. No indication of any injury. My skin is unblemished. No stitches. No mark.

It was Terrance who said it. I know he did. The day I woke up after the accident. He told me the doctor had a performed a "minor proce-dure." What kind of procedure, even the least serious, wouldn't leave some kind of scar? If there was no cut, why was the bandage on at all?

There's a knock on the door. I put my foot over the bandage on the floor.

Who is it? I call.

"It's me," Hen says.

She opens the door halfway. "Are you almost done? You've been in here forever."

I was taking a shower, I say. You off to bed?

"Yeah," she says. "Come say good night before you go."

Sure, I say. You got it.

I close the door behind her. Then I move back to the mirror and stand there for a while, looking at my shoulder, my back, my neck, my arms. The sensors he applied to collect data are still intact.

I don't know how long I stand like this. Until I've seen enough. Until I've dripped completely dry. My towel is untouched on the hook on the back of the door.

When I open the door to Hen's room, to our room, she's lying in bed. She stands but doesn't say anything. She closes the door behind me, then takes my hand and leads me to the bed. She takes off my shirt and lets it drop to the floor. She pulls my shorts down. She lays me down on the bed. She removes her shirt and then her shorts. She pushes her underwear down and lets it fall around her ankles, stepping out of it.

She comes onto the bed with me. She gets on top of me, straddling me. She puts her hand between her legs and guides herself onto me. She leans down, grabs my wrists, directing my hands, putting them on her back. I try to touch her face, but she pushes my hands back to where she'd placed them. She leans forward, resting her head on the mattress, to the right of mine. She puts her hands flat against the wall above the bed. She's moaning. I am, too.

We stay like this until she's done and rolls off, breathing heavily. We haven't kissed.

She's lying on her back, looking at the ceiling.

"Why do people stay together?" she asks a few minutes later.

In long-term relationships? I ask.

"In marriages," she says.

Because they love each other, I say. They're committed to each other. They depend on each other. There's comfort there, security.

"No. They stay together because it's expected, because it's what they know. They try to make it work, to endure it, and end up living under some kind of spiritual anesthetic. They go on, but they are numb. And the more I think about, the more I think there's nothing worse than to live your life this way. Detached, but abiding. It's immoral."

I'm not numb, I think. I'm not detached.

Marriage is hard, I say. Living with another person for years takes work and effort. You can't just give up when things are hard.

She rolls onto her side.

"I know you think what you're saying makes sense. And it might in theory. But I'm not talking about giving up when things are hard. I'm talking about forced survival when things are rotten."

When things are rotten, I repeat in my mind.

I hope you're not suggesting things are rotten between us, I say. I really hope not. Look at what we just did. You enjoyed that, didn't you?

She touches my arm.

"You don't have to worry about that. It was fine. It served its purpose."

Hen, these last few days I've been feeling something real for you. Something new and incredible. I can't describe it.

She places her hand on my stomach.

"Try," she says. "What does it feel like?"

There are so many things, Hen, so many things—objects, stuff, and so many people. Just think about the canola fields and all those flowers and everything living in there. The grain at the mill. And think about the city and everything there, the stores and apartments and vehicles. Think about all the screens people have. For almost everything, any object you can think of, there are too many. There's only one you, and it's miraculous.

She doesn't say anything but moves over closer to me, putting her arm around my waist. She leans in and kisses my bare chest. She stays like this, nestled into my side. I close my eyes. I want to remember this when I'm gone.

"I had a nightmare last night," she says several minutes later. "It felt so real. This one was especially bad. I was terrified right from the start. I knew it was a dream. I was lucid dreaming, I could do whatever I wanted, I could control it, supposedly. But that didn't make it any better. I was in this big room. I could see all the walls, I was aware of its size, but I also knew the space went on forever. The space was limitless, but I couldn't go anywhere else."

That sounds awful, I say.

"And the worst part—I want you to understand this—I wasn't alone. That's the worst part: I wasn't alone."

They're both in bed, asleep. Hen and Terrance. I should be, too. I don't know what time it is, but it's late. Middle of the night. I'm not tired yet. The house is quiet. Not silent. What I've learned sitting down here all night is that no house, even at this time, is ever silent, not if you're really listening.

I'm seeing things clearer now, sitting here in the dark, because my mind is sharp. I'm feeling more and more like my true self all the time, with every passing hour, understanding things about who I am, things I'd been neglecting.

Hen's comments on marriage got my mind racing. She told me about how she's feeling, concerns she has, but something in me knows that Hen and I are a team. We're better because of each other, despite what she said. That's what a marriage is. I should have told her that more clearly when she brought it up. We have different roles, different strengths, but we rely on each other. I can do what I do because I know she'll always be there. We need each other.

I'm the boat, cutting through the waves. Hen's the anchor. Hen is my anchor. My stabilizing force.

I push my recliner back and turn it around so it's facing the wall. I prefer it this way. If someone walks into the room now, they won't see my face immediately, won't know if I'm frowning or smiling, won't know if my eyes are open or closed. They'll have to walk over here, to the far corner of the room, to see me. Terrance, I mean. Terrance won't be able to see my expression. Not right away.

What's a boat without an anchor? It will get swept away, veer off track. At some point, it will be lost at sea. I should have said this, too, when we were in bed. It would have made her feel much better. I'm sure of it. To remind her of our attachment.

My theory isn't really a theory anymore. A theory is uncertain, whereas what I've uncovered has to be true. I understand this now. And I intend to prove it. Terrance isn't our friend. He never was.

Should I tell Hen or not? I wonder if she knows. The more certain I am that he's a threat, the less I want to tell her. It will frighten her, upset her, which is the last thing I want. She won't sleep. She'll worry.

I won't tell her. For her own good. What she doesn't know can't hurt her.

Terrance wants what I have. That's why he's living up on the second floor while I'm down here. Why he's cooking our meals, shopping for our food. Why he's going to my work. Why he's studying everything about me. He wants my wife. He wants my life.

I can't let it happen. I won't.

What's a boat without an anchor?

"Junior. Come on, Junior. It's time. Now. Let's go. Wake up."

I open my eyes. It's the morning. It's early. Barely light out.

Terrance is standing over me. He's not smiling. I'm not wearing a shirt. There is a suction cup sensor attached to my chest. What is this? Why is this on me?

"Junior. Can you hear me? What are you doing? Come on, let's go."

He looks different. What is it? He's not wearing his suit. That's what it is. He's wearing shorts, a short-sleeve shirt. Wait. It's my shirt. He's wearing *my* shirt. My shorts, too.

What are you doing? I ask.

He claps his hands together. "Junior, the morning's almost over. You need to get up now. You can't keep sleeping your last days away."

Why are you wearing my clothes?

"What? These? It's hot. I was getting too hot in my own clothes.

213

Hen suggested I borrow some of yours. She said you wouldn't mind. She said that you'd suggest it yourself, if you were awake. Now, come on. Up we get."

He leans down, and with his hands on my upper arms, helps to stand me up. My legs feel wobbly, and it takes a moment for me to stabilize.

"You said you had a busy day here, and I'm leaving now, too," he says over his shoulder, walking away. "There's breakfast for you in the pan on the stove. Make sure you eat. Take your pills."

Hen, I say.

I think of last night. I remember what I have to do, where my focus must lie.

Where is she? I ask.

"She's in the car already. And I'm off." He goes to the front door and right outside as I stand there watching.

I make my way to the window and look out. He gets in the car beside Hen. A minute later, I watch the two of them drive off without me.

I'm not the destructive type. But I have to do this. Things are beyond my control, and I have to do what I can to reassert some authority. It's out of necessity. For Hen.

He wants me to eat, so I don't. He wants me to take my pills, so I don't. He expects me to just do everything he tells me, but I won't. I won't do what he wants anymore.

It's taken some time to figure it all out. But I understand what I have to do to shift the balance. I have to prepare everything before they return home. I spend some time scouting around, checking angles. Then I pick the precise spot. It makes the most sense. I'll learn more from here than from anywhere else. That's what this is about—turning things on their head, learning, observing. It's about leveling the playing field. Why shouldn't I be able to observe, the way he does with me? This is my house. This is my life.

There are no do-overs. I can't fuck this up. Measure twice, cut once. It's not just about what I'll be able to see. It's about not attracting attention. I leave the bathroom and go back into Terrance's room. I look at the wall. I see the spot where I'll put it. I measure it, mark it. Then I go into the bathroom, which is on the other side of the wall. It's perfect—a spot between two cracks. Impossible to notice. Not unless you're looking for it, which he won't be.

I get my power drill. I bring it up to the bathroom. I'm nervous, anxious to get started. I will do it now. I turn the tap on in case someone comes home and wonders why I'm in here. It will sound like I'm washing my face, or shaving, or having a shower. All perfectly normal things to be doing in the bathroom.

I bring the drill to the wall where I want the hole to be. It's right above the back of the toilet. This is the spot. Already the shower's steam is filling the room. I've brought three bits with me. I'll use the smallest one first. I can always make the hole bigger if I need to. I take the bit out of the chest pocket on my shirt. My hands are shaky. I drop the bit before it's locked in.

I don't know why I'm so anxious. I shouldn't be nervous. This is my house. It's my drill. All this is mine. And this will be a small, almost invisible hole. There's nothing to it.

I wipe my hands on my pants and take a breath. I squeeze the trigger softly, barely starting it. The engine whines. It goes through the wall easily. I don't push too hard. I don't need to rush. It takes longer than I thought. But then I feel the wall give way. I take the drill out and blow into the hole. I bring my face up to it and look through. It's not a big hole but it's effective.

It's amazing how much you can see from such a tiny hole. I can see his bed. I can see his pillows. I can see one of his bags. Finally, a shift in the balance of power.

H ello, I say. Welcome home.

Hen has just walked through the door. She looks exhausted. Terrance is still out in the car. She stops when I speak. She looks at me.

"What are you doing?" she asks, studying my face.

I've been waiting for you guys, I say. It's good to see you. I'm glad you're home.

I walk over, lean in, and kiss her on the cheek.

You're my anchor, I think. The stability and assurance I need to be me.

"Junior? Is everything okay? You don't look like yourself," she says.

Terrance steps through the door. He's wearing my work vest, the one I leave at the mill. He looks from Hen to me. "Junior?" he says. "How was your day? Feeling all right?"

Yes, everything is okay, I say. I'm feeling fine.

"Here, take this," he says, handing me two more pills from a bottle he removes from a pocket.

I can feel them sitting in my palm. I don't say anything but pop them in my mouth. He waits, watching me until he thinks I swallow.

"Good," he says. "If you don't mind, I have a lot to do tonight, so I'm going upstairs. I'd like to interview Hen in a bit, too. Will you be okay on your own for dinner?"

Of course, I say. We're used to having dinner on our own.

He's already halfway up the stairs when he turns and asks again, "Are you sure you're okay, Junior?"

Fine, I say. Same as always.

And before I can say anything else, Hen follows up behind him and is gone, too.

This is precisely why I drilled the hole. For a moment like this. When he's in his room and thinks I'm oblivious. When he thinks he's in control.

I've calmly made my way upstairs. I sneak into the bathroom and close the door behind me. I'm straddling the toilet, hunched over the tiny hole in the wall.

They are sitting across from each other. Looking at each other. Face-to-face. The room isn't in darkness. There's light. Terrance is sitting on his bed, Hen on a chair in front of him that he's pulled over from the desk. He's closer to her than he's ever been to me in our interviews. And facing her. He never faces me. I can hear them, but it's not clear exactly what's being said.

Right now, she's doing most of the talking. He's typing into his screen, which is on his lap. He's nodding every so often. Twice he holds his screen up to her, as if he's taking measurements like he's done with me.

The sensor on the back of my neck is tingling. It started this morning, but I've been ignoring it. The sensation, one of warmth, as if it's purring, is increasing. I find scratching it helps. Scratching both the skin and the sensor itself. I'm scratching it now as I watch these two, this stranger sitting with my wife. It's hard to tell where my skin stops and the sensor starts.

I doubt Hen is fully aware of what's happening, the depth of his deceit. It's not in her to be deceitful, especially not to me. But whatever it is they're talking about, she has a lot to say. He's nodding. It's possible she's started to suspect something, too. She might even sense that I'm onto Terrance and am watching now, taking care of her, protecting her.

I made sure to pretend I swallowed the pills he gave me, but I threw them out as soon as he went upstairs. His drugs aren't helping. They're hurting. They aren't painkillers. I don't believe that anymore. I think they're affecting the way I think. I think they're meant to limit my reasoning, make me more vulnerable, more pliable, more obedient. The drugs have been slowing my intellect, numbing my intuition. He doesn't want me to figure out what's really going on.

She points at something on the screen. He nods. My head feels heavy. He puts his screen down and shifts forward in his chair.

He leans toward her. He puts a hand on her leg.

I can't watch this anymore. That is my wife. He's touching her. This has gone too far. I have to act. Before it's too late.

I stand and run out of the bathroom. I burst through the door, into the room.

S top, I say.

They both turn and look at me.

"Junior!" Hen says.

She looks more surprised than Terrance. There are tears in her eyes that I couldn't see from the hole in the bathroom.

I saw you, I say. I saw him. I know what you're trying to do.

I'm pointing a finger at Terrance. It's trembling.

This isn't okay. You've taken this too . . .

I want to say *far*, but can't get the word out. I feel a knot in my stomach.

"You don't look so good, Junior," Terrance says.

You're a bad man, I say.

My legs quiver. It's not right. I don't feel right.

"We're going to talk about everything," he says. "But now you need to calm down."

No!

I try to take another step toward Terrance but stumble and have to steady myself against the wall. Hen puts a hand to her face. Terrance takes a cautious step in my direction.

"Those pills in your system," he says. "They're slowing you down."

Painkillers, I say. You said they were painkillers.

He picks up his screen, types something into it, holds it up, takes a photo.

"Junior, please," Hen says.

I'm not waiting until Friday, I say.

My speech is coming out slower than I want it to.

I don't care anymore. I won't do this. You said Friday, but I won't let it happen. I'm not going to the . . . Installation.

I look at Hen. She doesn't appear scared or angry, but concerned.

"You don't have to worry about that," he says, setting his screen down on the bed. "It's time for me to tell you. There is no Friday. And there is no Installation. At least not for you, Junior."

It's the last thing I hear before I collapse onto the floor.

ACT THREE

DEPARTURE

I'm sitting downstairs in my chair, but I don't know how I got here. My chair has been moved back to its original spot. I'm no longer facing the wall. And Terrance is wearing his suit again.

It comes back to me. The spy hole I made. Me, taking a stand. For myself. For Hen.

"I'm sorry about this. I know you must be feeling . . . unwell, sluggish, confused."

He's wrong. That's not how I feel. Not at all. I can feel my heart. I'm alive. That's what I'm feeling. I'm feeling alive.

"The time has come, Junior. And I'm sorry I haven't been completely honest with you. Nothing in life is random or by chance. This has all been painstakingly planned and arranged for you. You passed the test."

I open my eyes. I blink. It takes a moment to focus. I try to move my head, but I can't. I want Hen. I know she's here, but I can't see her. Where is she?

"What's in your best interests, your well-being—these have been priorities from the beginning. You've done so well. It's amazing. You're amazing."

What the fuck is going on? My eyes are adjusting to the room. It's dark outside, but there are several spotlights on outside the house, shining through the windows. There are cameras around the room, several set up on tripods. And they're all pointed at me.

It's not until I try to move my arms that I realize my hands are tied. The metal bracket Terrance put on my arm is now attached by a chain to a second metal bracket that wasn't there before. It's on my other wrist. I follow another chain down in horror and it is connected to brackets around my ankles. I'm bound. I'm a prisoner. In my own home.

My wife, I say. Where's Hen?

"Shhh, you're okay. Don't worry. We're here."

I use whatever strength I have to hold up my hands. They feel impossibly heavy.

"There were other possibilities for how this would go, but in the end we felt like it made the most sense for you to be made aware at this point, and to see the end for yourself. Considering how far we've come, it's only fair. And it is useful for us, too, for our research. Our research is the most important part of this whole endeavor. We need to establish objective probabilities for future initiatives."

I already know, I say, I've figured it out.

My voice sounds hoarse, weak.

All of it, I say. I know what you're doing.

"Is that right?" Terrance asks.

You didn't want me to understand, but I'm smarter than you think.

He smiles. "Yes, I believe you are smarter than I think. I'm just not convinced you've figured anything out. Who am I then, Junior? Tell me."

The replacement, I say. You're my replacement. When I'm sent away, you want to take my place. You want to stay here with Hen.

"So you think I'm your replacement," he says into the microphone in his screen.

I hate him. I hate everything about him. He's recording everything I say.

Where's Hen? I ask. Hen needs to hear this, too. She needs to know.

"She's right there."

He points over his shoulder. I try to look beyond him. I see a small figure sitting in a chair. It's Hen.

"See? She's here. She's been in on this the whole time, Junior. She knows everything."

Hen! Don't worry, Hen, I say. I won't let anything bad happen. I'm not going anywhere. I promise. Hen? What's wrong?

She's hunched in her chair with her hands in her lap around her stomach. Why isn't she coming over to me? Did they chain her, too?

"I'm sorry," she mouths to me, and then releases her hands, bringing them up to her face.

I see now she isn't chained. She's free to get up if she wants. She's been holding herself back.

That's it? That's all she has to say? Just that?

I look at Terrance again.

You've been lying! When you take me away, you will take over my life. But I'm not done yet. I'm not ready to go. I won't let it happen! Get these off. I'm not your fucking prisoner. You can't do this!

When Terrance speaks, he's completely composed. "Can you tell me what you're feeling right now, Junior? Describe it. Physically, I mean. How's your head?"

My head? Why are you asking me that? Fuck you! I want these off!

I hear a noise outside on the porch. Talking. There's something out there besides the lights. Someone. Shuffling of feet. My front door creaks open. Two men, both in dark suits, walk in. They're wearing tight, dark gloves. They say nothing. They just stand on either side of the door.

What is this? I ask. Who are you? What are you doing in my home?

"Don't worry. They're with me," says Terrance.

Hen? I call again. What did he say to you? Why are you just sitting there?

"This way," Terrance calls toward the door. "Bring him in, please."

Bring who in? Who's out there?

Another man approaches. When I see him, something in me breaks. The feeling I have is unlike anything I've ever felt. Confusion mixed with anxiety that turns quickly into terror. I can't believe what I'm seeing. The man stops just inside the doorway and looks at me.

It can't be real. It's impossible. This can't be happening. But it is. There's no mistaking it. It's here. It looks so real. Not artificial, not manufactured. Lifelike in every way. Standing in my house. It's me, standing at my door, looking at me.

The replacement. My replacement. I'm trying to process what this means. Terrance wasn't lying. He's not taking my place. A replica, just like he said. It does exist. It's here.

I can't stop staring. I feel like I'm floating. I can't speak.

"Junior, I know how you must feel right now," Terrance says. "But please try to stay calm. Look at me. Here. Focus, please. Stay calm."

Terrance is speaking directly into his screen now. I can't hear what he's saying. I don't care what he's saying. He's irrelevant now.

What's standing in front of me is identical to me in every possible way. It couldn't look any more real or human than it does. I shift my gaze down to my own hands. The veins in my hands, the lines on my palms, my fingerprints. Aren't they unique? They are mine. Only mine. How can there be an exact replica, a facsimile of me? It's not possible.

"Hello," it says.

The voice. It's my voice. Not similar to my voice, but identical.

"Junior," Terrance says, "I want you to meet . . . Junior."

I feel a brief moment of wonder. The replacement eyes me. He gives me a slow nod. Suddenly I'm filled with a wave of anger. I don't want to see it. I don't want it here. Not in my house. Not with my wife. I don't care how real it looks — it's not real! It's not me.

No, I say. No!

"We have to take you away now," says Terrance, "But it's important that you were here to see this, to experience the reversal face-to-face. We wanted you to be part of this step, too, to help you process it. You're facing the truth now. Your own truth. We wanted to see how you'd react."

My truth is right here! I yell. In this house, with Hen!

"No, it's not. You're not . . . him. I'm sorry we had to deceive you during this process. I'm sorry to tell you: it's you. You're the replacement. He's the real Junior."

Hen? I shout. Hen!

I'm pleading with her not only with my words but with my eyes, with my whole body. She won't make eye contact with me. She's looking into her lap. She's just sitting there. Why won't she look at me?

I watch as the thing takes a step toward her. She looks up and is staring now, in awe. In awe of it.

"Hen," it says. "Hen."

"Hi," she says. She wipes at her eyes.

Shut up! I yell. Someone stop it!

It's looking at her. I can't take this. The feeling is much worse than anything I imagined.

"I can't believe it," it says. "It's you. I can't believe I'm here, Hen."

It's talking to my wife. Talking to my wife as if it's me, as if it's the real one. Talking to my wife while I sit here, tied up.

"It's been a long time," says Hen. "Is it really you?"

She stands, reaches out, touches it. She touches its face, its hands. Then it leans forward and kisses her. On the lips. She stands there. She doesn't stop it. It puts its arms around her.

No! We don't want this, I yell to Terrance. We don't agree to this! Get it off her! The deal's off! I'm not leaving!

Terrance walks over to one of the men in gloves, whispers something in his ear.

"You're not going anywhere, actually. You've been where you needed to be all along. Do you understand? You've already done your job. We're going to be writing about and talking about you for years. I brought you here on my very first visit, the day he, the real Junior, left to live on the Installation."

He nods in the direction of the thing that is standing with its arm around my wife.

"You won't be able to understand this, but that was the day your mission started, the day the real Junior left. You saw the headlights on my car, didn't you? That was your first conscious thought. That's how we devised it: those headlights were your actual beginning. After that, it was up to you."

That's not true, I say. You're lying. Hen, tell him he's lying!

"It is true," Terrance says. "You can't remember much from before your years with Hen. Am I right?"

He's giving me time to think.

"That was intentional. We wanted the present tense to be your focus. And any of those clear memories you do have of the past? Like the first time you saw Hen, your wedding, moving into the house, those years at work? We gave them to you. We spent many hours with the real Junior before he left, asking him about his life with Hen. We got those memories from him. They're actually his. They were important for him, so we made them important for you."

He points at the thing. I can feel all eyes on me. All of them in the room. Except Hen's. She must be terrified and upset. Confused. She must be as shocked as I am.

"I hoped by doing this, agreeing to it, that it might help us," Hen says. "Junior and me. The real Junior, I mean." She looks at the thing with its arm around her. "I thought while he was at the Installation, having a replacement of him instead of the real thing might help our relationship. I thought it might help me appreciate what I had before he left."

But I *am* Junior, I say. You know I am.

She shakes her head. "No," she says. "I'm sorry."

It takes a step toward me. "My god," it says. "I can't believe it's so much like me."

I want to lash out. The chains won't let me.

It comes closer. It bends down now, onto its knees. It's a few inches away, assessing me.

"It's unbelievable," it says.

It turns to Terrance, then to Hen. "I can't believe I'm actually back. I'm home," it says.

You shouldn't be! I yell. You don't need to be. Leave! Go! Now!

"Calm down," Terrance says. "It's time. We have to take you away now."

But this is my home! You can't leave him—that thing—with her! She doesn't want to be with it!

The men in gloves approach me from both sides. They each grab one of my arms, holding me down.

Don't touch me! Get away from me!

Terrance walks right up to face me.

"Before the end, I need to thank you for everything you've done," he says. "You are the first of your kind. There will be more, but you'll always be the first. Because of what you were able to do here, all on your own, for years, we know so much more now than we did before, so much more about what's possible. You did it. I'm so proud of you."

The thing looks down at me. "Thank you," I hear it say. "For looking after Hen while I was away. For helping her miss me, the real me."

I don't want to go! I don't want to go to space! I want to stay!

"You aren't going to space," Terrance says. "The first stage of the Installation is already complete. That's why Junior is back."

My breathing is so heavy now, from the heat, my bound wrists. I can't seem to catch a full breath. I feel as if I'm choking. I try to make eye contact with Hen, willing her to look at me, but she doesn't. She won't. She doesn't look happy. I know she doesn't. She looks upset. No one else notices, but I do. I know. She's not happy with him.

"Your work is already done. You did exactly what you had to do, better than we could have hoped. Junior has returned. And it's time for him to get his life back."

I can feel my nostrils flaring in and out with each breath. It's exhausting even holding my head up.

"Rest," he says, touching me gently in the middle of my forehead, just above my eyes.

Everyone in the room starts clapping. The horrific applause continues for too long.

"Is there anything else you'd like to say now?" Terrance asks.

More shuffling outside, bright lights in the window, feet on the porch, whispering.

"You've done all you can," he says. "It's time."

Time for what? I ask, using all the strength I can muster.

"It's time for this to end."

Where do we start? There's so much to say. So much to talk about, to discuss, to recount, to share, to explain. I thought about this moment often while I was away. I dreamed about it. I pictured us, right here, with me finally back home. I've been through a lot. I have so much to tell Hen about.

We had no communication, none at all, for the entire time I was gone, over two years. Two years, four months, three weeks, and a day, to be exact. That's a lot of time to be away from your home and your wife. So much to say.

Instead, we're sitting here at our small table, the one I built before I left, not saying anything to each other. Not the homecoming I was anticipating.

I cut a piece of potato, dip it in some sauce, and put it in my mouth. I smile as a chew. Things will be better than they were before I left. They will be, I tell myself. They have to be.

"I don't even know where to start," I say.

"Yeah," she says. "Me neither."

The commotion of my return and the departure of the replacement and Terrance and the OuterMore crew has left us exhausted. Especially Hen. She's aged. I can see it in her face and her eyes. She walks heavier than I remember.

It's understandable that we're both a bit overwhelmed. It was loud and busy, traumatic, too. It wasn't a real death, of course, but it was . . . something. They called it "induced fatal entropy." And there were so many people here. OuterMore staff monitoring, collecting, gathering information, measuring, reporting, a whole fleet of vehicles outside. I wanted them to leave as soon as possible when it was done.

Here we are again, the first time we've been alone in years. The silence can't go on. It has to be broken. So I break it.

"They weren't sure how I would feel, or even if I'd be able to walk for a while," I say. "Being up there for so long can have weird effects on the body. I still feel wonky."

"It looks like you've lost some weight," she says.

"I have. They had us on these treadmill things most days. But the muscles can shrink despite that. Without the pressure of gravity, your tendons, ligaments, it can take some time for the body to readjust. The next wave that goes up there won't have to worry about adjusting to life back here. They aren't coming back. The next wave is permanent."

Hen sets her fork down beside her plate. "It will take some guts to be part of that. To leave when you know you won't be coming back. To go somewhere that's inconceivable."

"It would take more than guts," I say. "Trust me. Nothing is familiar up there."

I know she is proud of me, proud that her husband was part of something as important as the Installation, a trial run that was physically and mentally taxing. But this is about her, too. She allowed me to go, and she waited for me while I was away, with that replacement to keep her company. It was quite a sacrifice to make, maybe not the same as mine, but it was something. I couldn't have done this without her.

"I took a ton of videos, but they won't do it justice."

"I can't imagine," she says, pushing her plate away. She hasn't eaten anything. She has just rearranged the food on her plate.

"You look like you've lost some weight, too," I say.

"It wasn't exactly normal for me down here, either," she says.

I nod. I don't quite know what to say. But if she can understand the difficulties I went through, then she'll feel better about things, about her sacrifice.

"It sounds stupid and obvious, but the word that comes to mind is *big*. Our space inside was restricted, but everywhere else, everything outside, was so big. Vast. It's weird. Instead of feeling part of an important mission, I felt cut off. Even living with those other people, on top of each for that long, I felt isolated. It's hard to explain. I missed home." I have to ask her. I've been thinking about it, but I haven't yet asked. "What was it like, living with it?"

She rubs her forehead, then looks at me intently. "You're asking about what I went through?"

She sounds so surprised.

"I guess so, yeah," I say.

"It was hard at first. Much harder than I thought. I barely said a word to it. I avoided it. It was just the two of us. It took a long time, months, but I got used to it. It could learn things and adapt. It started to become aware of me in a way I didn't expect. It was genuinely concerned about me. I know it was. We formed a bond—not the same bond as with you, but more than I would have ever guessed. After the first year, we would spend time talking, and it was clear that it wanted to understand me. It listened."

"So you felt a bond with it because of blind devotion? Programmed devotion?" I ask.

She's silent for a moment. "No, I wouldn't say it like that. And blind devotion is not what I ever wanted. I can't help but wondering why they had to shut it down. Why not keep him going after all he had been through? After all he'd learned?"

"You called it 'him' just now, you know."

"Did I?"

"Yeah. You did."

I put my fork down and wipe my mouth with my napkin. "Did you eat together every night?"

"Yes, we did. Of course."

I don't say anything. I'm hoping she'll elaborate.

"He wasn't you, Junior. He lived like you, he imitated you sometimes, but he wasn't you. I acted as normally as I could at the beginning, but it was strange. And the talking part, the behavior, that part was amazing to witness. It would react to things just as you would have. Sometimes, though, it reacted differently from the way you would."

"You mean better?" I say.

"I said different. That's all," she says.

"Before I left, they asked me so many things, to tell them memories I had from our years living here, details about our marriage, about you, things only I could ever know. They wanted such specific detail—things we said, things we did, anything I could remember. They must have used all of that, instilled those memories in it, even though my memories couldn't mean to it what they mean to me, to us. I guess I did it well, if you felt it behaved mostly like me. But when you say there were times it was better than me, what do you—"

"It wasn't identical. That's all. That's all I mean. And I didn't say better. You did."

I sigh, rub my face. I feel tired suddenly, worn out. "I take it as a compliment. I wouldn't want to be identical to some freaky living computer."

"Junior?" she says.

"What?" I ask, and it comes out loud and pointed.

"I think it genuinely cared about me, especially near the end. It didn't at first. It was just following its design, but by the end . . . I don't know. It felt like . . ."

"I think you're imagining it, Hen. OuterMore went over all this with us. They predicted you would develop a relationship with it, but it's not real. It's not a person. You sound like you've forgotten that," I say.

"The way it would look at me sometimes," she continues, "or when it would get annoyed or distant. I learned from living with it. It would listen."

"Hen, that's just the way it was made. It doesn't mean anything."

"Maybe. But it helped me. That's all I'm saying."

"Well, I guess that means they'll be happy with the results."

"You mean OuterMore?"

"Yeah."

"It seems a shame, though," she says.

"A shame how?"

"That it doesn't exist anymore. I wonder if it can be replaced. I mean, if you can be replicated and replaced, couldn't it be replaced?"

This line of conversation is starting to annoy me. I want to talk about me, about what it was like up there. That's what we should be talking about.

"Why are you worrying so much about your fake digital husband when your real husband is back? No matter what happened while I was gone, it's over. Now, it's just like old times again. It's just you and me," I say, leaning over to kiss her cheek.

She stands abruptly, gathers our plates, and takes them inside.

I finish the beer I had opened to have with dinner. I set the empty bottle down on the table and look out toward the field.

"You would have hated it up there," I call. "So lonely and desolate."

She doesn't reply.

"I won't leave you again. Imagine if you'd heard about this as a little girl—that one day you would have a part in helping your man do something incredible, be part of something historic. It would have been hard to believe back then, right, Hen?"

Nothing. No answer at all.

Change is difficult. She'll be okay. She just needs some time. It's all so hard to believe, to comprehend. Here I am, at home again with Hen. She's here for me. Her place has always been right by my side. She'll come around. She doesn't need any more excitement or drama. She's always been my anchor. She always will be, no matter what.

I 'm using the first week back to get settled into my life here. It's harder than I thought it would be. I probably shouldn't be surprised that it isn't the same as before. I was away for a long time. It would be impossible to think I could just step right into this life as if nothing had happened.

Work has been fine. I'm back at the mill. I spend my days bagging grain and seed. Mary asked about Hen's cousin, Terrance, but otherwise she doesn't know anything. Neither do any of the other guys. To them, it's as if I never left.

At the house, with Hen, things continue to feel unsettled. The house itself isn't in great shape. There's a lot of work to do around here. I'm taking my time to chip away at the chores. Today, I'm repairing a large dent in one of the baseboards in the living room. Hen's in here, too, on her screen. She was already in here before I started. She doesn't offer to help or even ask what I'm doing. It irritates me, but I decide not to say anything. I'm doing a lot on my own these days. And I wasn't the one who let the house get into this state.

"I shouldn't be too long," I say. "Just trying to make things nice around here."

She looks up from her screen for a second. She doesn't say anything. I leave the room. I go down to the cellar to get a piece of sandpaper. When I return, her screen is still there, but she's gone. I pick her screen up off the table. It's locked. She's set it so it won't open without her fingerprint. That's new. It never used to be this way.

W e're lying in bed. It's dark. I've been up here for a while, attempting to fall asleep. I'm trying to keep as regular a routine as possible. I go to bed at the same time and get up at the same time. Hen came in a few minutes ago. She's late to come to bed. She used to go to bed whenever I did. But I don't mention that.

She doesn't say anything, just gets under the sheet and turns away from me. But I can tell she's not asleep yet.

"What is it?" I say, frustration in my voice. "Is there anything you want to tell me?"

"No," she says.

At least she's not arguing. She's been like this more and more since I've been back. Instead of improving each day, getting closer to me each day, she seems to be drifting, more closed-off, more internal, colder, and distant.

I get up, walk down the hall to the bathroom. I splash a handful of water onto my face and look in the mirror. How did they manage to make it look so much like me? I open the medicine cabinet, and something moves and then falls out. It's a bug, a big one, one of those horned rhinoceros beetles. Before I can step on it, it scurries under the vanity.

I head back to our bedroom, back to bed. "I saw one of those big beetles," I say when I'm tucked in. "The big ones."

"There are more and more of them around all the time," she says. "More than before you went away. I didn't like them at first. But you get used to them. Now I don't even notice them."

"I don't think I'm going to fall asleep," I say a few minutes later. "I'm thinking about things."

This is my blatant attempt to start a conversation. But she doesn't pick up on it. She doesn't ask what things I'm thinking about. She doesn't turn around. She doesn't say a word.

"What do you want?" Hen asks, surprising me.

I'm standing at the fridge, the door open. I thought I was in here alone.

"You scared me," I say.

I'm completely caught off guard by her question. I've been back over a month, and Hen has barely spoken to me, barely asked me a question in days, maybe even weeks.

"What do you want?" she asks again.

I straighten up, swing the fridge door closed.

"A snack," I say. "I want a snack. And I'm getting it."

"I don't mean from the fridge. I'm talking about this. Us."

I should have figured it would be a question like this—aggressive, laced with anger, demanding.

"I have what I want," I say. "I don't just mean the snack, either. I mean this. All of it. I don't want to go anywhere else again. This is it."

"So this?" she says with her arms raised in the air. "This is enough for you?"

"I don't know what you're getting at. I'm the one who *had* to leave, while you got to stay home. It wasn't easy up there, Hen."

"Do you ever think about what my life is like—before, during, after? Does it ever even occur to you that I don't exist to look after you? You're oblivious, and you can't even see that I've changed."

"Of course I can," I say, "And I hate it. I hate it like this. I want you the way you were before, Hen. That's what I want."

"Is it? Is that really what you want?"

"Yes," I say. "You've been living with a monster. It's over now. Can't you just get used to that fact? I'm back. We have everything we need right here, and I'm not leaving again, ever. You don't have to worry about that. We have our life back."

"No," she says. "You have your life back. This is the life for you."

I'm expecting her to continue, to say more, to yell. Instead, she leaves.

"Hen!" I call out after her. "Did you fuck it?"

I hear the front door open.

And then it slams shut.

I wake up out of the blue. I'd fallen into a deep, restful sleep. Lots of elaborate dreams. I've been out for several hours. It takes a moment to realize I'm alone. Hen's not in bed beside me.

I reach out and put a hand where she sleeps. Cold. Did she even come to bed?

I see a light, a glow from the window. I walk over to see what it is. It's a fire. A small one just outside the house, but it's a fire. Hen, she's out there. I see her standing back a few feet, looking at the fire.

"Hen!" I call. I run down the stairs and out the front door.

"*What are you doing?*" I yell as I approach the fire. I've grabbed a shovel off the porch and start hitting the burning object at the center of it. It's wood. I try to break it up, throw dirt on it to put it out.

"Are you crazy? You have to get ahold of yourself, Hen!"

I kick a chunk of burning wood with my boot. It's her piano

bench. The bench I made for her. Years ago. She must have brought it up from the cellar.

"What the fuck are you doing? Why burn the bench?"

"Sorry," she says. Her eyes lit up. She's still glaring into the embers. "I should have told you." She's won't look at me.

"You need to get a grip. I'm serious. You're dangerous and destructive! Look at me . . . we can't go on like this!"

"You're right," she says. "We can't."

I go to work. I come home. I eat. I feed the chickens their grain. I sleep. Routine has returned to our lives, but it took many months too long.

There are a few more chores to take care of, some inside, some outside. We eat dinner, sometimes together, more often I eat alone. Most evenings, we sit in different rooms, watching different things on separate screens. We do it all over again the next day.

But I've reacclimatized. I've adjusted to this new normal. Physically and mentally. There are few surprises. I'm not complaining. I've had my share of excitement—enough for a lifetime.

The arguing is over now. Stasis has set in, and I'm fine with that. The quiet is not so bad. I'll always take silence over bickering and shouting. Neither of us has the energy for that anymore. Hen has her ups and downs, but who doesn't? Nobody's perfect. And no relationship is perfect.

I come to on my own, opening my eyes. It's morning, still early. The first trace of daylight is shining in the open window. I love this time of day. It might be my favorite.

I stretch both arms above my head, and stretch my feet, too, off the bed.

"Good morning," says Hen.

I turn over. She's sitting in the chair against the wall. She's dressed but has a red towel wrapped around her hair as if it's still wet. I can't remember the last time she said good morning to me.

"How long have you been sitting there?" I ask.

"A little while, not too long."

She looks well rested, relaxed. Composed. At ease.

"I'm glad I'm not working today," I say. "I might just stay in bed a bit longer."

"You should," she says. "Why not? I have something for you. But I'll leave it on the counter in the kitchen."

"For me? Can't you give it to me when I get up?"

"No," she says. "I'm going out."

She stands and rubs both hands on either side of her head before taking the towel off. She hangs the damp towel on the back of the chair.

"Bye."

"Yup, see you later," I say, pulling my pillow over my eyes.

I sleep in much later than I'm used to. I didn't think I'd fall back asleep after Hen left, but I did. I had a sex dream about her. We fucked right here on the bedroom floor. We were all over each other. When I wake up, I wish she was beside me so I could make the dream real.

I think our brief but pleasant exchange in the early morning put me at ease. It might be a small indication that she's coming around, that she realizes she has it good here. I have nothing planned for today. I don't need to leave the house. I can putter around at my own pace. It's a day meant for me.

Hen put the coffee on before going out. Another thoughtful gesture. I pour myself a cup and lean against the counter. I'm about to take my first sip but stop. I'd forgotten what she said until right now. She was going to leave something for me. That's what she said. And there it is, sitting on the counter beside the coffeemaker—an envelope with *Junior* written on the front.

I set down my cup of coffee and pick up the letter. I grab a knife from the drying rack to slice open the envelope. Inside is a letter. Folded up. I take it out. I straighten it, turn it over in my hands.

It's so strange. There's nothing written on this note. Nothing. Front or back. The page is blank.

I 've spent the entire day outside, mostly in the barn, replacing some shingles on the barn's roof and putting fresh wood chips in the nesting boxes.

When I walk back inside, I see Hen. She's sitting in the living room with her back toward to the door. She's looking out the window. She was gone all day. Eight hours, maybe longer? I didn't notice her come back, and she didn't tell me.

"You left a note," I say. "This morning before you left. It was blank."

Before I can say anything else, Hen speaks, without turning around.

Look, she says. We have a visitor.

I glance past her, out the window to the road, where a car's green headlights light up the lane.

Were you expecting anyone? she asks.

"No," I say.

We watch the black car drive all the way up to the house. It parks out front. A moment after the engine stops, a door opens. Terrance steps out and walks to the porch. I head to the front door and open it just as he's about to knock.

"Junior," he says. "It's great to see you. Hello, Hen."

I look back over my shoulder. Hen is a few feet behind me. She has her hands clasped in front of her. She's grinning warmly at Terrance.

Hi, she says. It's nice to see you again.

"What are you doing here?" I ask.

"It's been a while since I saw you, Junior. I wanted to pop by to check in on you—on both of you. To see for myself how things are going. Once you become part of the OuterMore family, you're part of it for life," he says.

Would you like to come inside? Hen asks.

"No, that's fine. I see that you're all set, that there aren't any problems."

We're fine, says Hen. I was just about to get dinner started.

"And, Junior? You feel the same way? Everything is fine?"

I make eye contact with Hen. "I'd say things are finally getting back to normal, yes."

I believe this as I say it. Hen smiles at me. I feel the affection in it, the enthusiasm. As of right now, I feel like maybe we've turned a corner. That Hen has acquiesced.

"I won't take up any more of your time then," he says.

Thanks for coming by, Terrance, Hen answers.

"I'm glad you're doing well," he says. "Best of luck to you."

T hankfully, Terrance's visit was a brief one. If he was worried, he probably would have stayed longer. He left satisfied.

I find Hen in the kitchen, standing by the stove. She's cooking something in the pan.

"How'd it go today?" I ask. "You were gone for a long time."

I step closer and wrap my arms around her waist.

She turns to face me. She kisses me on the lips. I take a step back.

What's wrong? she asks.

"Nothing. That was nice. I'm just . . . a little surprised."

She doesn't say anything but kisses me again, longer this time.

I'm happy, she says. I'm happy here. You make me happy.

"That's the best thing I've heard in a long time," I say. "Hey, should we eat outside tonight?"

Yes, she says. If that's what you feel like.

We sit across from each other. We eat and drink and talk. She asks me how things have been at work, asks about some of the repairs I'm making around the house. I tell her a story about a machine I repaired at the mill and explain to her how the machine works and how I fixed it. She's full of questions and listens intently to my answers. She laughs at my jokes.

When we're done eating, Hen doesn't get up and take her plate into the kitchen the way she has after pretty much every meal we've had since I returned. We actually keep talking. It's what we used to do when we were first married.

"I have to say, this is a pleasant development, Hen."

You mean dinner? she asks, taking a sip from her glass of wine.

"Dinner, yes, but I mean everything tonight. Just this. You. The way you are tonight. You haven't seemed yourself lately."

Really? Since when?

"Honestly, pretty much the whole time since I've been back. You've been so distant. It's like you've been living in your own world."

I know, she says, putting down her glass. You're right. I'm sorry. I haven't been myself. But today, I feel much better.

"Really?"

Yes, really, she says. I'm here for you. You know that, right? I like it here, and I want you to be happy.

It's a relief to hear her say it. It's what I've been waiting to hear since I returned home.

"I want *us* to be happy," I say. "Together."

Of course, she says. We'll always be together.

I put my hand on hers.

"Forget what I said the other night, at the fire," I say. "I was just frustrated. I'll make another bench for you, for your piano."

Thank you, she says. I'd like that. I'd like to start playing again.

She stands and stacks our plates.

Want anything from the kitchen? she asks.

"Maybe another beer," I say.

Okay, and when I get back, you can tell me more about the Installation. I want to hear everything.

She takes our dirty plates and leaves.

It's a strange thing. The way we're interacting tonight has made me feel younger, lighter. A weight has been lifted. Tension can build up and live and fester, creep into in the smallest corners of daily life. This a move back toward regularity, to predictability. We all want certainty. And we have it here, everything we need.

I've taken to walking around the house in bare feet since I returned. We were never permitted to take our socks off on the Installation, other than when showering. Now I never wear socks. My feet are a bit dirty, but I don't mind. I like it. I like feeling the old wooden planks under my feet.

I could sit here forever. That's how I feel tonight. It's a beautiful evening. Beyond the canola, the sun is dipping low on the horizon. The only thing missing is Hen. She should be out here with me. There's still so much to tell her. What's taking her so long? I wait a few more minutes before getting up.

I find her in the kitchen, standing in front of the sink. She's not moving at all. She's stone-still. I don't think I've ever seen her stand this still before.

"What are you doing?" I ask.

She doesn't reply. She doesn't move. She's standing there, transfixed.

"Hen?"

She's looking at something in the sink.

"Hen! Hello! Henrietta!"

This causes a reaction. She raises her head, turns, brushes the hair from her face, looks at me, and smiles.

It's really interesting, she says. It's not moving. It's just sitting there.

"What are you talking about?"

Sorry, she says, I didn't forget your beer. I just got . . . distracted.

She walks over to the fridge, grabs a bottle, opens it.

Here, she says, handing it to me, kissing me on the cheek, and walking outside.

I stand there for a few seconds, pleased by this welcome sign of affection—another affirmation that Hen's back to her old self again. Her true self.

I walk over to the sink. I look in and recoil. I'll never get used to seeing them. There, beside the drain, is another one of those disgusting horned beetles. That's what Hen was staring at.

Using a spoon from dinner, I crush it against the bottom of the sink. It crunches under the metal. You have to get rid of them, all of them. They don't belong here. Nasty things. I let the water run, washing the remains down the drain.

I set the spoon back down where it was and head outside to watch the sunset with my wife.

ACKNOWLEDGMENTS

Nita Pronovost, Alison Callahan, Samantha Haywood, Kevin Hanson, Jennifer Bergstrom, Jean, Jimmy, Lauren Morocco, Adria Iwasutiak, Felicia Quon, Sarah St. Pierre, Meagan Harris, Brita Lundberg, Stephanie Sinclair, Barb Miller, Ken Anderton, METZ, Florettes+2, Iceland, Charlie Kaufman, everyone at Simon & Schuster Canada, everyone at Scout Press, everyone at Transatlantic, my friends, my family.

Thank you.